T0196351

MOUNTAIN AIRPORT

MOUNTAIN AIRPORT

SEAN MCDONAGH

MOUNTAIN AIRPORT

iUniverse books may be ordered through booksellers or by contacting:

iUniverse
1663 Liberty Drive
Bloomington, IN 47403
www.iuniverse.com
1-800-Authors (1-800-288-4677)

ISBN: 978-1-4917-8859-2 (sc)
ISBN: 978-1-4917-8858-5 (e)

Library of Congress Control Number: 2016902994

Print information available on the last page.

iUniverse rev. date: 10/17/2016

CHAPTER 1

The Pas, Northern Manitoba, 1986

The jukebox was playing "Running Bear," Johnny Preston's version, from which John Cardinal had received his nickname. John, who was Dan Owen's native co-worker, laughed and participated along with the gang in their mad exploits—silly, youthful stuff that kept the town constable always on the lookout for what might happen next. The whole gang of friends was dancing at Mulligans bar when they decided to take a couple of twelve-packs to Indian Lake and indulge in a midnight dip.

The atmosphere at smoky, rowdy Mulligans was thick enough to cut with a knife. The place was packed with people of all shapes and sizes, all slightly drunk. So deafening was the noise that no one could hear anything unless someone literally shouted in his ear. Dorothy had her arms around Dan's neck. "Let's go swimming," she said, and Dan just grinned at her. As the beer was being paid for at the liquor outlet, John said, "Race you round the log road, man!" to Dan, who grinned and jumped on his Harley-Davidson. "Back shortly!" he shouted to Dorothy. John and

Dan tore off on their two-kilometre race, both wanting to win and quickly return to join the others. They were riding speedway-style, sending dust flying through the air. Out of nowhere as they banked around a corner, a logging company grader appeared.

Dan braked as hard as he could to avoid the monolithic mechanical scraper but needed to drop his machine to do so. He tumbled off into the brush. As he looked up, he caught sight of John slamming into the side of the grader and flipping through the air. The frozen image seared into Dan's brain. Dan quickly jumped to his feet and ran over to John's crumpled body. He held his hand while John exhaled his last few breaths. Heartbroken, Dan drove as fast as he could to alert the ambulance, hoping there was some chance that John could be saved. But the ambulance attendants soon pronounced John dead at the scene. It was deemed an accident. The grader driver was criticized for not having lights on, but in June at The Pas even at eleven in the evening, the light could still be reasonable.

Dan had known Running Bear since both were five years old. They'd had to be separated in a fight just before the morning school bell rang. They had walked home the same way and growled at each other for thirty seconds before sharing a stone to kick down the road. By the time they'd reached their respective homes, they were firm friends, a friendship that extended into both families. Rarely was one seen without the other. Each had the other as backup as they grew and got into fights. They always dated girls and went around as a foursome. As they grew into their youth and early manhood, both had developed laid-back, humorous personalities, and both were attracted to the town girls, who reciprocated their attraction. Neither was violent or nasty; between them, they always treated women with the utmost courtesy and respect. They regarded everybody as a friend unless someone broke that trust. Some regarded their friendliness as weakness and tried to belittle them, soon finding out they were mistaken when they were on the wrong end of a fight they'd picked. They had both started work at the pulp and paper mill as labourers, as many people did, and soon their experience of the whole process allowed them to specialize on one part, which gave them a better rate of pay.

They had two summers out in the brush, camping, fishing and riding around on newly acquired motorcycles. Running Bear had an old Honda 150, and Dan an even older—much older—Matchless 600cc, which was new in 1950. Running Bear found much merriment; if the advance and retard mechanism on the Matchless was not set perfectly, the kick-starter would often kick back, sending Dan skyward. The next summer both met significant others. Dan met Dorothy, and Running Bear was sweeping Saffron off her feet.

Dan could still see, and would continue to see, Running Bear's grinning face as they each slid around the corner into the path of the grader. Running Bear's girlfriend, Saffron, was crushed with grief at what had taken place. It was just too much for her take in, but she, along with John's family, could not be spared the devastation, such pain. Dan sought out Running Bear's father to give him an account of what had happened. He was mightily relieved not to be wholly blamed. Yet Dan could feel the heartache of the man who'd loved his son dearly.

Dan knew that if he had answered, "Race you another time," or something like that, then Running Bear would be here now. Dan's girlfriend, Dorothy, sensed his devastation as Dan started a slow drift in and out of depression.

Eventually, time being the great healer, Saffron met someone who was instrumental in helping her through her grief spiritually, where counseling had not helped. Saffron was never judgmental with Dan, but a distance, a rift, between them appeared, though neither wanted this. They both felt awkward in each other's company.

CHAPTER 2

The Pas, Northern Manitoba, 1992

It must have been six o'clock in the evening when Dan Owen took off from St. Andrews Airport in Winnipeg. Dan did not get along with the guys at Winnipeg and was openly hostile and sarcastic to them. They in turn regarded Dan as a drinker and a cowboy flyer and thought him dangerous to himself, his passengers and anyone else in the sky at the same time. They had contacted the company that Dan worked for that owned the aircraft to let them know of their misgivings. The officials had told Dan there was to be an official inquiry regarding his sloppy landing a few weeks ago, when he'd arrived with three members of the Swampy Cree First Nation. All of them were the worse for wear after a big lunchtime beer session. The landing was made worse by one of the occupants opening the door as the plane landed; he pushed out 20-odd empty beer cans that clattered along the runway. Previously, enraged by what he deemed a condescending attitude by the flight controller as he radioed in to land, Dan had aimed his Cessna at the control tower and screamed obscenities as he came within

25 feet. He overshot the airport and landed at Pidgeon Lake, a few miles away. There was mayhem in the control tower as everybody ducked and dived. Another transgression. He had been careful to wait till dark and leave his 15-can case of beer where he could pick it up before leaving. He filed his flight plan and headed out to the twin-engine Otter parked near the apron. A security camera flashed as he walked to the plane after coming out of the washroom where he had hidden the beer. No maps in his case.

He took off in the twin Otter, a beautiful full moon somewhat veiled by a mystical cloud, and headed toward The Pas, taking the plane to 6,000 feet. He had to deliver a relay for the mill that was urgently needed. He let the autopilot take control. Good, he thought and left the pilot seat to relax in the cabin with a beer. He would see his old buddy Bev Miller at the Pas, transfer the relay to him and then head to the Legion for pickerel, fries and beer. It would take less than a couple of hours to reach The Pas, but he was already exhausted. Within five minutes, on his second beer, Dan fell into a deep sleep.

He had a weird dream that he was falling, out of control, air rushing around all him. Suddenly reality burst upon him when he was thrown forward by the angle of the falling plane, a rude awakening. He quickly realized what had happened and jumped into the pilot seat. He fumbled for the fuel reserve switch and the safety harness. The plane was descending rapidly in a spiral, and he was below 1,500 feet, the stall warning system beeping its loud shrill. The radio was alive with the voice of his friend Bev Miller.

"Dan, Dan! Over, Dan!"

Dan tried to restart the engine. Almost immediately it

fired into life, and all the lighting and control panels burst into illumination. Dan put the nose of the aircraft down and accelerated until the engine was screaming. Glancing at the altimeter, he saw he was below 1,000 feet and knew he had to act quickly and positively. He managed to stop the spiral and level out. Having recovered the stall he leveled off and took stock of where he was. His heart was pounding as he wiped the sweat off his forehead. Planes this old were not supposed to be treated like this.

He relaxed as the plane leveled out and turned to his compass. Then he spoke to Bev. "Okay, Bev, it's me. I just had a little wobble here, but I am okay now. Can you give me a fix?"

Bev gave him a compass heading to The Pas. "I have been calling you for half an hour," said Bev. "You are halfway to Thomson. How much fuel you got?"

Dan looked at the calculation gauge. "Reserve tank only," said Dan.

"You're good then," said Bev. "No big headwinds, so you should be fine. I will track you back … What happened?"

"I just lost concentration. I must have drifted off," said Dan dishonestly.

"Okay, partner. You are 35 minutes away, and its beer and fish at the Legion tonight. Sure you got that fix okay?"

"Oh, I can find the Legion okay, Bev. Ha ha," joked Dan.

"How did you get there? You're way out in the boonies, Dan," said Bev.

Bev knew there had been a major incident up there and began to craft a parable that he could repeat to Dan. He enjoyed his friend's company and did not want to lose him. They had worked at the mill together, and Bev volunteered as an air traffic controller. There were reports via British Columbia/Manitoba and Alberta airports of Dan's indifference to flight rules and his penchant for beer while flying.

Dan landed the Cherokee at The Pas and taxied to the quiet, empty control tower and parked. He joined Bev, who was waiting patiently in his truck, and they shook hands. As they entered the Legion, Bev said, "Get me one, Dan," and offered Dan a twenty-dollar bill, but Dan waved it away.

"Think I owe you more than just a dinner tonight, Bev."

The Legion held a raffle on Friday nights, along with a pickerel dinner, which was very well attended by many of the inhabitants of the small town. Dan had worked at the pulp and paper mill at The Pas for two years in his late teens and knew many people living in the town. Soon they would call the raffle ticket numbers, and the lucky winners would go home with loads of steak or fish. Most people fished in the pristine lakes around The Pas, where there was a variety of fish. Many people at The Pas engaged in ice fishing. Many had moveable shacks that could be towed onto the ice. The shacks had a hole in the center where an ice auger was used to drill a hole in the ice. Then a line was sent down with a baited hook to tempt any nearby pickerel or trout. A wood stove kept the occupants warm, and there was beer and rum to slake the thirstiest of thirsts.

Bev picked up the Legion microphone and blew into it. "Testing, testing. Good evening, folks. We have a distinguished guest with us tonight ... none other than that old gunrunner to the Irish, Dan Owen!" A laugh went up. "Is he okay here in the Legion, Don?" Bev said to the

Legion manager. "Sure there's a cease-fire now, and we want our split on all that money he made!"

Dan grinned at the gentle ribbing he was taking as he walked back to the table with two big plates of pickerel and fries. As he arrived he felt a hand on his arm and turned to see an old flame. "Dorothy." He smiled. Dorothy had been the love of his life for two years before he met Diane. She was absolutely lovely in the short dress that showed off her superb hour-glass figure.

"Howdy, stranger. What's happening? What's going on?" she asked. "Go eat your food and save me a dance." She beamed at him, and he beamed back.

Dan and Bev ate their fish and drank their beer before Bev touched on the earlier incident. Dan said that he was tired and fell asleep. Bev, as kindly as he could, mentioned how many aircraft had crashed in northern British Columbia, Alberta, Saskatchewan and Manitoba with their bad weather and difficult flying conditions. Dan nodded and said he was about to begin a fitness regime to offset the tiredness. Which he was not.

Bev worried about Dan's health. He seemed to be losing weight fast, and his disposition seemed desperate. Rumors about his beer consumption and antics abounded.

Dorothy and Dan had their dance, but she was aware that he was different: no sense of direction and seemed a bit boozy and lost. She had heard that his marriage to Diane was in trouble and that he was drinking too much but said nothing. She was an old married lady now. Her husband was also at the draw and had met Dan. Best leave the past as a distant and wonderful memory. Dorothy had been with Dan the night Running Rear died and had witnessed the change in Dan after the death. Then he'd moved to British Columbia. She guessed that was the root of his problem.

The next day Dan looked up some friends on the reservation to check out how things were going. They went fishing in the late afternoon. Dan was sad that he could not stay longer. The Indian Day Festival that Dan had been to many times previously was the following week. He'd enjoyed the wonderful dancing, foods and artifacts that were available. The dancing seemed to epitomize the Cree culture and their struggles and always left Dan feeling warm inside. Many Cree people, also known as the Ojibway, were hunters, firemen during the summer forest fire season, mostly started by lightning, and guides for the US hunters who came up to visit in the summer and autumn.

On Dan's backhaul to Winnipeg, he carried two passengers and just drank tea. He arrived without incident.

CHAPTER 3

Vancouver 1990

atalie lay in a Vancouver hospice, terrified, as her lungs slowly evacuated the fluid trying to drown her. Another bout of coughing subsided, allowing her to breathe again. She was suffering from ALS (amyotrophic lateral sclerosis). Her depression and anger at where she found herself were not tempered by the humiliation she felt at being cornered by the legal reality that did not include a remedy or solution that would help end her horror. She simply had to wait for her condition to worsen to the point that coughing could not clear the phlegm seeping into her lungs. She wished for the dignity of choice and an end to the massive discomfort and fear. Her doctors were doing their level best within the confines of what, by law, they were allowed to do.

"Please," she said through clenched lips as another bout came on. The nurse lifted her into a sitting position as her body convulsed. Blood and phlegm pooled around her mouth and chin. She had become incontinent and hated being changed. She dreaded her life, one she used to cherish so much. There was nothing to look forward to, only to dread. In many ways, the courts and the law were responsible, not for the fact that she had ALS but for insisting that she run the course of a frightening and painful death. Life was changing, and it seemed that corporate structures, for good and bad, were taking over elected officials but in parallel rather than by votes. The lobbyists for the evangelical right were in effect controlling the courts via their propaganda. There would be no mercy for people dying in agony while the Old Testament corporate-sponsored organizations held sway. Wars like the one in Iraq, where governments were used by shady religious and arms manufacturing lobbyists, with thin excuses offered for their piracy. Dusty bombs in inventory had to be used somewhere. Many families lost loved ones within the military and civilian populations.

Natalie's niece, Emma, cried and sent an implored look at the doctor, while Dan looked on stoically and held his aunt's hand. The coughing continued. As Natalie's struggles increased, it seemed obvious that she was losing the battle to stay ahead of the game. "Please," she gurgled again, and Dan said "Do something!" The doctor had already made up his mind that the threshold had been passed and immediately put a needle into her arm, injecting a large dose of morphine. The coughing stopped almost immediately, and a slight smile appeared on her lips as Natalie lapsed into unconsciousness without fear of death ... just life. Fr. Smyth and the niece and nephew huddled, and then he administered the last rights. The doctor updated the chart with the final report.

Dan gave comfort to his cousin Emma. Both were upset. He repressed the anger he felt at how the medical system treated, or was forced to treat, its patients. That evening in a Vancouver hotel Dan was seething as a politician on TV defended the government's assisted suicide policy, stating that only God had the right to take life and that they were defending the weak against those who would take life. Dan wondered how the politician would have fared in his aunt's situation.

CHAPTER 4

Memphis, Northern British Columbia

emphis, a working town, was the most northern location in British Columbia, Canada. The Rockies provided a wonderful backdrop and a skiing facility. The town had a specialist pulp and paper mill that had operated since the 1930s. A metallurgical coal mine sent coal, mostly via train, to Prince Rupert on the West Coast, where it could be shipped within four days to its biggest customers in Asia. The Japanese, Chinese and Indians loved the coal from this part of the world; its efficiencies for steel making were legendary. They got a much better bang for their buck with Memphis coal. The town had around five thousand souls and lots of eateries and restaurants, many of them with different cultural menus that mirrored their immigrant culinary themes infused with Canadian flavors over the years. In the evening the town center buzzed as people milled around the restaurants, bars, fast-food outlets and the cinema with two screens. There was talk about reviving the drive-in movie facility that had shut down 10 years earlier. There were lots of outdoor activities in both summer and winter. For people living in Memphis, summer time was camping time. Workers headed into work on Friday mornings already loaded with provisions for taking off Friday night to head out into the bush, preferably by a river or lake. Once there, the beers in the coolers were quickly opened, barbecues lighted, and burgers seared. People liked to meet others while camping or go in groups. All over western Canada people headed out to the hills. The weekends were about fishing and relaxing with the family till the return Sunday night or even early Monday morning. There were no big box stores. Instead, medium-sized outlets sold clothes, shoes, jewelry, tack, food. There was a Ford/GMC dealership, and two cultural shops sold moccasins and other First Nation crafts made on the reservation.

In the winter, people rode snowmobiles and went ice fishing, skiing or snowboarding. There was little excuse not to be outside in Memphis, and children there were bought up that way.

Memphis was an old town and small enough, so most people knew most people.

Dan and Diane had got together after Dan was transferred from the mill in Manitoba, when they were both twenty-five. Both Dan's parents had passed on by the time he was twelve, and he had been bought up by his Aunt Natalie, along with his cousin Emma. They had been introduced at a company dance, and Diane was captivated by the slim, tanned individual with shaggy hair and blue eyes when they danced together. An unexpected pregnancy had firmed up the relationship rather than love. Neither knew at that time what love was, but there was tremendous attraction, and that was enough. She liked his bravado and swagger, characteristics that had long ago diluted or disappeared. Then he'd had more electricity and was fun.

He had eyed a 650cc Triumph Bonneville motorcycle and was considering purchasing it to replace his Harley when he sensed that his gang of friends was moving away from that lifestyle into newer relationships more to do with pairing into couples and camping and fishing. Motorcycling had long been losing its attraction anyway. He did not often hunt but tagged along with those that did for a weekend, and Dan became proficient at skinning and butchering wild meat of all sorts.

Diane's parents initially and then for some time loathed Dan, who they regarded as slightly thuggish and without many, or maybe any, social graces. With the birth of their first grandughter, they had reluctantly acknowledged and tepidly accepted the relationship. Dan and Diane had moved into an old bungalow that was pleasant enough and would be improved as time went on. A second child was born, a boy, completing their family.

Dan continued to work at the paper mill, running the mill digester system. He had settled into a routine. He had leaned to fly to better serve his ambitions of working with or for a survey company. He gave himself two to three years to realize his ambition. He had a natural flying ability and mastered flight in all situations. Dan could fly in the mountains and flew when most would not take off at all. He knew how to shelter from the centers of storms. He was also instrument rated for night flights and over any terrain.

Dan had purchased an older bargain Piper Cherokee Cruiser light aircraft. He obtained LiDAR mapping skills that were much in demand by geologists for high-resolution maps. As the LiDAR, which stands for Light Detection and Ranging, mapping work increased, he worked through a survey company for one of the many mines in northern British Columbia, Alberta, Saskatchewan and Manitoba. Dan was happy that much of his work came through a geological company that had its own aircraft, which meant that he flew much more sophisticated machines than this own very basic 1970s Cherokee Cruiser. He also took other LiDAR work when it was available, and along with urgent part deliveries and ferrying people, he soon found himself busy all the time. Dan left the pulp and paper mill as his workload increased and formed his one-man company.

His relationship with Diane had settled into one where they slept in the same bed, but over the years they had been together their relationship had become functional. They were thus somewhat distant but close enough to survive. Diane accepted things as they were but wished and sensed that not only was there something unspoken between them but also a part of him that she was not allowed to see, an aspect that was possibly even unknown to him. It was like part of him had died. He has shouted and lashed out at a small starving dog that approached them looking for food, and she wondered why. Also, Dan had always liked to drink, but it seemed to happen all the time now. Diane knew a tragic accident had led to the death of one of his friends a few years before she met him and wondered if that was bubbling away in his mind eating away at him.

Dan was moody, and while he understood that, supposedly, he and his family were doing well with his newer flying business, there seemed a chasm in his spirit that he could not understand, a feeling that he was about to understand something but could not grasp its meaning. It felt tantalizingly close but still out of reach.

Diane was seeing an improvement in Dan as the workload increased and he seemed happier. She wondered if this would continue as, although they were far away where she felt they needed to be in their relationship. She was helping him with the growth of his Flying business doing the accounting and scheduling the work and there seemed to be a balance in her life of being a Mum and having a part time job. He had also talked of a family holiday but had not said where or when.

Cub Peterson had offered Diane a big discount on any parts she would need and she told him she would check it out when she needed some. She did not altogether trust Cub or his real reasons for wanting to do business. He was known as an individual who always wanted to get his way and would resort to other methods if his questionable charm failed.

But life was good today and Diane looked forward to seeing her friend Marlene for coffee that lunchtime.

CHAPTER 5

I t was on a mapping survey flight, when bad weather had blown him off course to a very remote part of the mountains, that he had first flown over the dilapidated airport. It fascinated him to see an old control tower, other buildings and a runway in a place so remote. Dan flew over the site half a dozen times, mesmerized to find anything in this remote location, especially an airport. He took a fix on the location and decided to visit it but keep his discovery to himself. At the first opportunity he headed north on an ATV to explore his find. It took days to get there, and Dan was glad he'd bought enough fuel and provisions. The terrain, even in high summer, was difficult to impossible.

The disused airport was only just recognizable. The runway was covered in debris, and the long-silent towers were quiet. He was totally enamored by the unexpected situation as he began to explore. Two large windows were broken, which allowed easy access, and he passed gingerly through to discover a large reception room with furniture in place and a kitchen just behind. Maps were still pinned on notice boards, plus some pictures of WW2 aircraft that once must have taken off from there. But where would they have been going to from this mountainous British Columbia location, he wondered. The stairs up to the control tower were rotten and had collapsed, and many spring/summertime nests had been built and then fallen into disarray. He could see from outside that at the other end were two locked doors leading into offices. Fascinated, he planned to return to view them properly when he was better prepared.

He returned to the airport later in the summer, armed with tools to make a survey and to better explore his find. The airport was not visible to overflying commercial planes because they flew too high, and only his mapping work and bad weather had led him into that area in the first place. He had told no one about the abandoned airport he wanted to explore better. It was about a three-hour flight from Memphis but not in an area people would want to visit. He had an ATV and trailer, and it took two days to get there through valleys and forest.

British Columbia was the most beautiful place in the world, with its ancient Douglas fir, cedar forests and vast untouched valleys. When he arrived, he found the place was undisturbed, and he wondered about bears and cougars that might be in the area. He had researched the situation in the combined library and museum in Memphis and believed the WW2 airport was one of a string built toward the end of the war to face the new threat from the Soviet Union. Missiles from both sides and long-range bombers soon made such tiny airports obsolete. So the tiny vestige of WW2 had been shut down as economically as possible and soon forgotten. By 1947 world was tired of war, and a new and different type of energy was being pumped into society, both industrially and socially, for people to enjoy the fruits of their labour and enjoy life without conflict.

He entered the locked offices via a window he managed to pry open. It was clear that he was the first being in there since it had been abandoned. Desks, filing cabinets, tables, chairs and a bar stood as they had been, albeit without beer. All paperwork had long gone. Further exploration led him to a maintenance bay that was badly weather-beaten and a dormitory and ablution block where the roof had collapsed. The whole setup could have hosted more than two or three aircraft and a dozen personnel. He decided to make this a camp where he could settle overnight. He felt it secure enough to leave provisions and equipment. He began work to shore up the office area, using the bar as his kitchen. He made it as comfortable as he could. He intended to bring up as much propane as he could carry and install a gas fridge and also bring a small Honda electric generator, a small electric stove and two wood stoves. The scenery was just beautiful, and this site was just what he needed to recharge his batteries, to inject some purpose and vision into his spirit. Never in all his days in Canada had he seen such a valley, with fir trees that stretched out before him at the cliff end of the runway. It was a wonderful lost world. He'd had a terrible year with family problems and drink and had been devastated by the loss of his aunt who had bought him and his cousin up and the manner of her passing.

The following year he had his airport camp ready and began to consider how he could fully utilize it. By fixing a small plow shield onto his ATV he had sufficiently cleared the short runway and thought if he wanted to build a hunting lodge there that could be a plan for the future. His accommodation was secure, and he had many of the comforts of home, including a fridge, mostly full of beer, a small cooker and a rudimentary shower. He had also stocked canned food, dried vegetables, longer-life bacon and both powered and fresh eggs. He had lights and a very basic landing-light system consisting of solar battery–powered flashing lights, like the type used to define roads for open-cast mining, controlled with a fob, that allowed him to fly to and land at the airport if he wanted to. The main office was designated as a communal bedroom for now, and the wood stoves were for cooking and heat on cooler nights. He wanted to see of there was any water nearby. He soon discovered a natural well in a rock formation with pure sweet water. So his airport now had a kitchen with a gas fridge, a basic shower, a sheltered living/sleeping area and a latrine. Not the Ritz but functional, he thought. Dan intended to revert the bar and kitchen back to being more of a bar and intended to bring up plenty rum and whisky to accompany his beer, though ice might be a problem.

His newly acquired pastime of hiking and snowmobiling had aroused interest among his family and friends. He'd never seemed the sort to evaluate and wonder or to appreciate the beauty and abundance of nature's scenery. Diane wondered if he had met someone else, but there were no other signs, so she was glad he had found an interest.

Dan had decided he would take his family there over the summer and decided to save the announcement as a surprise.

CHAPTER 6

Dan had never taken sick time from work, except for a few flu days over the years. Over a period of a few months he became strangely lethargic and felt weird pins and needles in his arms, legs and chest. He had no stamina but doggedly kept going. The strange sensation in his arms and legs was thought by the nurse at the outpatient clinic to be neuropathy, but it persisted and then worsened. Diane forced him to seek the advice of a doctor. Blood tests and a scan were carried out. After a three-day wait he was called at his work and asked to go to the doctor's surgery as soon as possible. As Dan walked into the office Dr. Meers turned to him and said in his distinctive South African accent, "Sit down, please, Dan. We are struggling to properly diagnose the problem, but from the physical tests and blood tests plus your family medical history, we believe you have a type of ALS. Please take a little time to take that in. Remember I am here for you 24 hours a day."

Dr. Meers prescribed the only approved medication, Rilutek, which along with some exercises would slow the progress of the disease. Dan was stunned. He was to begin treatment accordingly and immediately.

Dan went home. His head bowed, he put his arms around Diane. She burst into tears as Dan told her that ALS was diagnosed. She wanted a second opinion.

The onset of ALS had obviously caught him by surprise, even though he knew his aunt had recently died from it. Dan was scared that he might end up like his aunt. He was unable to communicate his feelings in any way with his family and friends, and the conversations with his doctor were short and to the point. Dr. Meers tried to speak person to person with Dan but was rebuffed, so he thought Dan indifferent and unemotional. He stuck to the facts and advised about dos and dont's. There was much confusion in Dan's mind as to what to do about this. He felt that he had choices, but the reality kept coming back to him that this was reality. There were no options except acceptance. It was what it was, and that was that. Once he allowed the icy water of acceptance to wash over him, he thought more about how to cope with it than if.

As Dan's condition deteriorated, it came evident that he could not remain at home long. Tiredness and a faltering stamina followed quickly, and a form of ALS without definition took grip. The thought of his aunt's passing haunted Dan. Diane tried to get closer to him to offer comfort. She told him that they were all rooting for him and said that she would be with him all the way. She thought better than to express her devastation about the news. There had only ever been him in her life, and the impending loss of her partner was something that would have to be dealt with day by day.

Dan was appreciative but unable to formulate a reasoned response or to say anything meaningful. Even his dad-in-law, whom he had never seen outside family events, visited him. He tried and even arrived with beer. The embarrassing meeting finished after 20 minutes. Dan was uncomfortable at home. He felt almost claustrophobic and had nothing to offer and didn't communicate with people. It was as if he needed to learn a new language. He felt he had turned into a complete loser.

Dan began to think more about leaving this world. It was suggested that he be moved to Vancouver for better treatment, but the thought of going back to where his aunt had passed on left him cold. He opted for the local geriatric care hospice and decided to put together a strategy, a plan, to remain the decision maker when it was time to leave God's earth. Dan had his own ideas. He would finish the job himself. He began to formulate a plan for an exit strategy. His mountain camp was perfect for that. He already had fuel, food, and some drugs up there, and he could "borrow" more from the geriatric unit. He would fly to his mountain retreat and die as and when he chose.

Without fanfare and with relief, Dan moved to a local geriatric hospice. He hated the circumstances, but he was a little more relaxed there without the guilt he felt at home. At home he felt like a loser, in his mind unable to offer what his family needed and had always needed, which he was unable to give. Danny Junior was into hockey like most kids of his age, but it was Mum rather than Dad who more often than not was present at the games.

He could see how strapped for cash the hospice was because of underfunding. He grudgingly understood the humiliation of losing all choice and lingering in what he regarded as hell's waiting room for death. It only needed the grim reaper, complete with hood, gown and scythe, to complete the illusion.

A confused elderly patient, a man in his seventies, felt threatened and kept nurses at bay with a knife. A young police officer arrived and tasered the 75-year-old man, not having bothered with any communicative persuasion. The young officer incurred Sergeant Squire's wrath, but this seemed to be life nowadays: no management, leadership or common sense. No time for a more human approach, no money for the real necessities, but plenty money and tax breaks for large companies and people well off enough not to need them.

Dan began to amass a stash of pharmaceuticals he'd purloined from wherever he could. He had a volume of strong painkillers. Morphine had been the most difficult, but he had claimed a supply, enough to see himself off when the day came, plus a syringe and needle and other general medical supplies. He felt sorry for the orderly from whom he had taken them and wondered how he had squared the missing items with the pharmacy.

Dan's fear of death was secondary to the manner of his death. Was it cowardice *not* to want your family to see you fall apart? Was it cowardice to keep control for as long as possible before deciding to drink a glass of whisky and reach for your gun? Was it cowardice to leave them with memories that were not all about the end? He thought of Father Smyth. Religion? He was never strong on that but believed that there was a God. He was not prepared to believe that we did not have choices between good and evil. Many traditional religions did sterling work in the community with the poor and those in need of help, even if all had their quota of child abusers and low-lifes. The evangelical zealots hated just about anyone who was not compliant with their brand of lunacy, which was why they hated things like insurance for all. Much better to sell the drugs at a vastly increased cost rather than deal with developing countries who could not afford them, leaving a vast amount of people dead.

Dan waited till nearly eleven in the evening before lifting himself out of bed. He had asked earlier for a drip to be removed because it was uncomfortable. Dan looked around his room and realized that he was leaving what many would regard as a cozy world to fly off into the blackness and cold, with the high possibility of not returning. He had eaten a relatively big dinner that evening, unsure about when the next meal might be, if at all.

Dan had not wasted time between his decision to fly to his hideaway and entering the geriatric facility. He had flown twice, keeping his condition as secret as possible, and delivered two shipments to the airport. They included all sorts of canned foods and beer, crates of Jack Daniels and rye, clothing, CDs, batteries, gas, tools and equipment, and what pain medications he had. He also bought up more practical items, such as soap, towels, and tissues. His mind was set, and he pushed himself to go through the motions and carry out his plan as he had envisaged multiple times in his head. He pushed the possible consequences out of his mind. His clothes waited in the bedside cabinet. He threw them on and dragged out his boots. He had no socks but knew all the cold-weather stuff he needed was either in the plane or up in his mountain hideout. He had one last look around and then snuck down to a lower level, easily avoiding the night attendant, who was watching television.

On his way down he became aware he was not alone. Two patients, both in very poor condition, were following him: Tony McPhee, a boxer with advanced ALS, and Ali, an alcoholic immigrant who had been in Canada for 25 years and was currently dying of liver failure. He would be lucky to be alive next week.

Dan angrily whispered to them, "What are you doing? Where are you going? Go back! Go away."

McPhee said, "I cannot stay here any longer, and it's the same for Ali. We've been watching you. You are making a break for it, and we want to come."

"No," said Dan. "You don't break out of hospital. I am simply leaving." .

"Please," said McPhee. "Take us, man."

Dan wondered how they had tumbled him. He had been so careful.

There were muted sounds in the distance. Dan's mind raced. He did not want the responsibility for these two, but he needed to move now.

"It's a one-way ticket," said Dan.

The distant sound grew louder, and Dan said to them both, "Come on." They slipped through a fire door and quietly closed it behind them. "Keep quiet," said Dan. They moved some distance from the unit before Dan turned and faced them both.

"I am going away. I am flying into the mountains, and if I can land at an old disused airport I know up there, then I am going to die up there. I am not coming back! I may not even be able to find it in the dark. I may run out of fuel and crash straight into the rocks!" Thinking they might be dead in a few hours seemed to bring McPhee and Ali to a stop. McPhee said, "I have no one here anymore ... an ex-wife and a daughter who rightfully don't want me. I do not want to die in a hospital. If we don't make it, then it will be quick.

"Me also," said Ali.

Damn! thought Dan, but if he were to go, it would have to happen *now. What the hell!* At least with them along his secret was secure.

He wondered what it would be like there in mid-winter. He expected to be dead by Christmas. He had a gun in case of attack and could always use it on himself it came to that but the thought left him cold. He would feel different he was sure if he was further down the road and in much pain or sufficiently weakened so that life had little or nothing to offer. He wondered also about what healthy people who take their own lives feel? How desperate would you have to feel and why? Maybe mental disorders where a voice kept talking to you uttering unpleasant of horrific things and would not let you rest. Maybe you were about to be ruined financially or morally and you could not stand the shame of this in public or privately. Maybe you lost someone who, the thought of living without was impossible, too much pain? But with the right drugs or support from family and friends many of these things could be fixed. It must be that people just could not see any hope from where they stood at that time. Dan felt a wave of compassion as he realised this reality and also a sense of admiration for the people on the suicide telephone lines and doctors and hospital workers who helped such victims over their problems.

But his was not a case of suicide. It was, to him, an

enforced action where there was no choice. He did not want to die but was dying anyway! It was a matter of, of, of what? Was it a matter of sticking your fingers up at the world in general? Was it a matter of telling the doctors that you were in charge of your life not them, especially as they wanted to get every last vestige of pain and suffering out of you. Was it really that you did not want your loved ones to see you suffer? Maybe a percentage of some or all of these feelings.

CHAPTER 7

The escape was easy, as easy as calling a cab and being left at a small mall next to the airport. They quickly covered the distance and ducked under the front gate. Dan knew there would only be the local volunteer air traffic controller at the airport, and although he would almost certainly see them take off, there would be nothing that could be done by then. It would be too late. The hospice would not realize for hours that they had absconded, maybe not till morning. *So here we are … action time.*

The night was chilly, and the dark, dark sky was suddenly threatening and scary. Dan felt cold and a little sick with worry. As the enormity of the task rammed home, anxiety was not just creeping but rushing in waves through him. He might never feel warm again. He grabbed hold of himself as the reality of never going came home hit him. A drip had been still running through him only hours ago. He knew he had to carry on with the plan now. The grass was slippery beneath his feet as he made this way over to his Cherokee Cruiser to begin his escape. The plane was fully serviced and topped up with fuel. The plastic cover was stretched taut over the cockpit and around the propeller.

Having neither the time nor energy to properly remove it, he pulled out his razor-sharp pocket knife and slit the cover. He tugged it free from the plane. The Cherokee Cruiser glistened in the cold night air.

He felt very cold and afraid as he fetched the keys from his pocket and opened the passenger door. Ali and McPhee slid in. It was very cold inside. He broke two hand-warming sticks and pulled out his pencil torch. It took no time at all to locate the premixed mickey of rum and take a deep swig.

"You do realize you could both be dead in a few hours?" Dan told them squarely. "If the lights don't come on at the other end, then that's it." Dan ran his index finger across his throat to emphasize the point.

"Let's go. Get that heater on," said McPhee.

The next part of the exercise required precision. Dan needed to quickly go through the pre-flight operations in an unusual mode. He had to wait to start the engine until there was an incoming fight. There would be one or two incoming flights but no more. His canvas bag held all he would need medically, but now he had two others to share it with. But he felt confident about his ability to get where he needed to go. He swung outside to do an aileron and rudder test and quickly check for a flat tire or whatever. He quickly made his pre-flight check of ailerons, rudder flaps and trim, and he checked both tanks for fuel with a dip gauge to make sure they were still full. He had 50 US gallons, enough with the reserve for about 550 nautical miles.

"Shut that door!" hissed McPhee. The three of them were very, very cold.

Thoughts about the enormity of what he was doing and the effect it would have on Diane and his two children ran through his mind, but an engine approaching from a few miles away was audible, and Dan knew it was now or never. The idea of lying and dying in a hospital bed as ASL robbed him of any movement or dignity, forcing his family to watch his horror unfold piece by piece expanded his determination. On their visit yesterday, he'd hated seeing his two wonderful children looking at him, neither they or he knowing how to communicate in such circumstances. Diane talked about normal stuff, like there was nothing wrong, which was her way of coping. He'd hugged and kissed Diane and his two children and waved goodbye. As they left he gripped her arm tightly, perhaps an unwilling giveaway of his intentions. Diane had rounded on him, their eyes catching, but he said no more, and she left, not sure what it meant but guessing something other than the obvious was amiss

The rumble of the incoming aircraft grew louder. As Dan jumped into the plane, a black shape jumped in before him, yelping and whimpering. It disappeared into the back of the fuselage.

"A dog!" called Dan angrily. "Get that fucking dog out!" he shouted to McPhee, who tried.

"Can't get anywhere near it," said McPhee.

The incoming Cessna approached, and Dan knew it was now or never, dog or no dog. He moved to choke the engine and hit the start button. The engine turned over smoothly and caught fire. He had a quarter throttle with a rich mixture. He would like to keep her running for 5 to 10 minutes but knew he had only around 90 seconds before the other aircraft landed. Old Cedric, even though he had a hearing aide in one ear, would soon wonder where the second engine noise was coming from. He saw the other aircraft land and taxi over to the control tower as he moved the console forward. The choked Cherokee slid forward, aimed for the tarmac runway. Now there was no more need to hide. Dan turned the lights on and set the plane for a medium to long takeoff, warming the engine, heading with a full tank down the runway. The plane lifted off the runway. He immediately set the compass and autopilot to the heading he wanted. Dan was ecstatic! So many times he had done this in his mind, and now it was for real. He took another swig of rum and set himself to his task. He knew where they were going and how to get there, but it was still frightening. He was still annoyed about the dog and wondered how he had acquired such a plane-load when he'd expected to be alone.

The dog hid at the back of the fuselage in the body structure.

Cedric ran outside and shouted at the Cessna pilot, "Who the hell is that? They are taking off with no flight plan. It must be a thief!" The Cessna pilot could offer no explanation. Cedric ran back inside to alert the local constabulary, headed by Sergeant Squires. There had never had such a situation in Memphis.

The plane lifted off, and Dan heard Cedric desperately shout into the radio, "Ten-thirty flight out of Memphis, who you are? You have no flight plan."

Dan quickly switched the radio off, not wanting to converse with the controller and also not wanting his thoughts distracted. He knew what his coordinates needed to be, and his navigation was preset due north from Memphis. His transponder was turned off, so no one would know where he was. He swallowed another mouthful of rum and passed the mickey over to McPhee, who swallowed and passed it back. For the first time in a long time, Dan laughed, holding the mickey skyward to salute what he deemed his escape. The journey would last around three hours. He pushed thoughts of problems that could occur. out of his mind. Things were fine *now,* and that was as good as it was going to get *now.*

Get your mind together, he told himself. Feeling he was in control of the situation, he turned around, grinning at his two companions, who, with frozen stares, tried to grin back. Flying was a terrifying experience in these conditions and warranted another swallow, which Dan and McPhee duly took. Dan offered a drink to Ali.

"Nope, not anymore," said Mohammed with a laugh. "I have had my last drink," he said. "Any more life I have will be a bonus, and I have no time for drink."

Dan laughed with Ali.

"Got any beer, Dan?" asked McPhee.

"Nope, not here anyway," replied Dan. "Got plenty at our new home," He grinned, leaning back and passing the mickey to McPhee.

"If we ever get there." McPhee grinned back.

CHAPTER 8

"Well, which plane was it?" Squires asked Cedric. "We certainly do not have many stolen planes around here."

"It's was Dan Owens's plane," said Cedric. "You know— that guy up in the hospital dying from MLS."

Squires shook his head. "I think you mean ALS," said Squires, who then left to file his report and visit Dan's wife.

Diane took a call from the hospice and was perplexed as the telephoned message sunk in.

"Gone? Gone where?" she asked the night nurse as the doorbell rang. "Just one minute," she said. She opened the door to see Sergeant Squires standing there with a bemused look on his face. Diane waved Squires in and went back to the phone. She hit the speaker button so that Squires could hear.

"Well, where could he go?" she asked. "He must be there somewhere."

"His plane's gone too," Squires interjected. "Was he well enough to fly?" he asked.

"Don't know," said the orderly. "But I would think not."

Diane was bewildered. This was far too much information to process, and there was no logic to it. How could a man with no more than a few months to live manage to get out of hospital and fly off? She felt deep anxiety run through her.

CHAPTER 9

The Cherokee flew on for nearly three hours. Dan put new batteries in the remote control, which was crucial for being able to see the runway.

He had set up lights at the airport that were both battery and solar-powered. Most mines used such lights on the mine roads. They should be good for months when activated, and he had the activation fob with him. He just needed to fit it into a remote and hit a button. The signal would switch his landing lights on at a range of 250 metres.

As they flew through the black night, Ali looked out the window and wondered what the odd light shining through the dark desolation meant. Perhaps a remote mine or fishing camp? He thought about how his life had landed him up here but pushed the thoughts away. He had already handed himself over to the Almighty and was at peace in his mind.

Ali loved Canada. He had studied Canada minutely when he arrived and delved into its history. He was fascinated by the Louis Riel era and Canada's evolution to the present. He did not stick to his community at all but was still thankful for his initial upbringing in Pakistan by his wonderful parents. His country was in the grip of the cancer of corruption and always had been. It was on its knees, and the "democracy" was such that it was impossible to stand up and shake off the corruption that was at every level. He loved Canada and felt an affiliation with the Trudeau-style Canada, all canoes and beaver-tail hats, camping and freedom. He had been intoxicated with Canada and unfortunately with alcohol as well.

Ali had been in Canada for 18 years and was now dying of alcoholism. He was totally dependant on alcohol in any form. It held a grisly fascination for him. He had been in the clinic many times and had been told over a year ago that he had had his last drink, but it had not stopped him. He was waiting to die without a drop of beer, and he needed constant monitoring. He should have been in an intensive care situation wires running out of him everywhere.

Alcohol had not been able to totally diminish his wonderful attitude to life and people. He'd been born to a pauper family in Pakistan, his early childhood and growing up full of abject misery. He'd found relief when he qualified through a scholarship to be an intern in Canada. He had worked well, and the company sponsored his application to become a permanent resident. You could not hold Ali back. There was so much to do and see, plus the relaxed social attitude to freedom—and the women! People here took him for what he was, a human being; it was as simple as that. He would never go back. He completely embraced the Canadian lifestyle and called himself Joe. People loved his cowboy hat and jokes, which when told with a Pakistani accent seemed hilarious. People laughed with him, not at him.

Ali's love of alcohol quickly turned into a dependency that he could not control. After 10 years he found he was building his life whole life around drink. Out of bed by three-thirty in the morning, he was in the office by five, having already drunk two double rums and swished his throat with mouthwash to cover up. Everyone thought that he was conscientious to be in so early to catch the Eastern clients. Joe worked furiously at his surveyor's position till around eleven, when he left for liquid lunches with clients who enjoyed his company. He spent afternoons writing reports with the assistance of a half bottle of rum until he was overcome by sleep. The evening session ran from six until he again fell asleep. Alcoholism demanded to be addressed by three-thirty in the morning, so the cycle would begin again until finally his liver gave out. The warnings were few, and his ability to squarely face them with a spell in the hospital only heightened his desire for more drink. His doctor gave him two to three months of life unless he gave up, but Ali could not believe that and carried on till he arrived in intensive care with no chance of recovery.

But Ali never did have another drink as the plane headed to the mountain airport. He had decided that the die was cast and that he would make peace with himself and God and enjoy whatever was left in his life. He was the closest of the three to death and needed to adjust mentally to his decision not to be tethered in a hospital but to give his ending to nature and feel free.

Dan was thinking forward and weighing up the possibilities. He had known the risks before leaving the sanctuary of his hospice but had gone forward anyway. He had no more than three months on God's earth, and he chose to close out in the mountains, either by landing or crashing to his end. It should take around another hour to arrive, he thought, and it suddenly dawned on him that in an hour his life, or what was left of it, would be changed forever.

The GPS was telling Dan that he was ready to go into landing mode, so he went down to a thousand feet and emerged from the clouds. Conditions weren't excellent but good enough. As he dropped below seven hundred feet, he hit the remote and straight away observed the lights that would guide them to the runway. A rush of adrenalin coursed through him.

An anxiety attack hit Dan. Was there debris on the runway since he had last been there? What if he misjudged the distance for landing?

What if, what if, what if! *Just do it!* he told himself.

But he now had other things on his mind. He aligned the plane with the lights, ready to land. All the lights were on one side of the tower so he could orient the aircraft.

A voice inside his head hammered at him. *What if you'd never put those lights in for cloudy conditions? You'd be a dead man! How would you like to be guessing in the dark right now during a night landing? How could you walk away from your wonderful family just like that?* "Well, I did put the lights in, and we are where we are!" shouted Dan. Ali and McPhee wondered what he was talking about and to whom.

Barely controlling the fear that enveloped him and resisting the panic running through him, Dan gritted his teeth and concentrated.

The craft was lined up, and he could see to the end of the runway. He took one more swig of rum and concentrated as the craft quickly lost height. He brought it in for a two-point landing and let the nose wheel settle on the runway. *A textbook landing.*

"Yes!" he shouted. McPhee whooped, and Ali laughed. Then the plane shimmied a little and was caught by a crosswind, forcing Dan to hit a rock with his right wheel, bending the strut. He braked hard, and the plane went into a spin, but he managed to bring it to a halt. A cheer went up. As they all looked at each other, grinning, a whimper came from the back of the aircraft. "The dog," said Dan malevolently

Memphis was abuzz with rumors about the disappearance of the three men. Search parties were out, but with there was only one conclusion—suicide. "There was nowhere for them to go," Squires said at a news update. Conspiracy theories abounded about the plane's disappearance.

People were perplexed. It all appeared so tragic.

CHAPTER 10

She looked at her watch and left home for her coffee date with a society of support from the school that Cub had mentioned when they were letting off their respective children at school. When she got to Tim Hortons, only Cub was there. Diane had left her children with their grandparents that evening; she would not have agreed to go if she thought just Cub would be there. Peterson knew Dan, and though they were not enemies, they certainly were not friends. They had different interests. Peterson had also known Running Bear, having being flattened by him all those years ago at a dance at The Pas. Cub had had too much to drink and had been rude to Saffron.

Peterson was well off with his transportation company and vehicle franchise and had recently divorced his wife, Sandra. Peterson was secretly jealous of Dan and had long coveted Diane. He saw this as his chance. Petersen regarded himself as a man's man, a tough guy who liked to get his way. Cub pretended astonishment that only the two of them had turned up. He'd asserted that there were supposed to be many others attending to exchange stories. Diane had gone with the thought that she needed to at least look at ways to rebuild her life. She was a very beautiful woman, with long dark hair, brown eyes and a freckly face with full lips. She had a superbly shaped body and did a little exercise; she was naturally fit. But there was no electricity and no chemistry, just a fumbled attempt by Cub to get another date going, to which she replied that she would see how her week went. "The kids, you know." She had only viewed this coffee date as a way of connecting with other single parents and was a little put out at Peterson's briskness and lack of charm. He seemed to want to impress her with his tough-guy image. She believed he had arranged this meeting just to get her on her own.

For her family, she wanted a proper life, and that had not happened with Dan's demon-drink dependency. His disappearances into the wilds and mountains for days at a time made her wonder if he'd met someone else. Now he had disappeared for good as far as she could tell. There were no textbooks to explain how she was to carry on with her life.

In Manitoba, the situation had been on Bev Miller's mind since it happened. He had been over to British Columbia, and while he was perplexed, he thought the three patients had not taken off just to fly into the side of a mountain, which was what most people thought. He puzzled over the direction of flight and where it would take them. There was nowhere to go!

CHAPTER 11

an had had to improvise with accommodations at the airport. He quickly started a large fire in two outside units and got the generator running for light, hot water and some heat. The dormitory had undergone basic repairs and would easily accommodate three people, as would the rudimentary ablution block.

The realization of Ali's advanced condition came upon them quickly. "Anything I can do?" said Dan as Ali lay on a foam mattress covered with a duvet.

Ali held up his hand and smiled. "No," he said. "Maybe tea?" McPhee joined the conversation. "Well, Joe? Did we do good by joining Dan or were we better off in the hospice?"

"Definitely better here, Tony. I can breathe here but I hope the food is not as bad as at the hospice." They both laughed.

"Don't know what you're laughing at. You have not tasted just how bad my cooking is," joked Dan. Dan played "The Passenger" by Iggy Pop on his CD player, thinking it an apt song for the occasion.

The kettle was slowly boiling on an outside wood fire, and soon Ali would have his tea. Dan had supplied tea, loads of green Japanese Sencha/Matcha tea that he was happily addicted to—along with beer. Dan thought about the practicality of ablution and how to best allow each man his own en-suite space. Hot water was not going to be a problem, but although there was plenty of cold spring water within 50 metres, he had only catered for one. Water would need to be carried over that distance. Maybe he could devise a fundamental pump now there were three people to look out for.

The dog had made its way out of the plane and, as if its emotional radar was homing in on where it could get the best deal, made a beeline for Ali. Ali laughed and said, "Nice dog," as it snuggled up against him.

"I know that dog," said Dan. "It's a little female stray that's always hanging around town. A real pain." The dog looked nervously at Dan and McPhee.

They needed to settle in for the first night. His gas fridge operated well and was good for keeping beer and food at temperature. Dan knew that within ten days up here the temperatures would be down as far as the minus 40s. He knew Ali would not last more than a few days. McPhee was in the 45th month of his ALS. He was certainly past his ALS sell-by date. His swallowing was difficult, and Dan wondered how all this would play out. *Well, who knows?* He grabbed a beer from the fridge and gave it to the boxer. "Some situation, eh?" said McPhee to Dan, grinning! "At least we are in control. What drugs you got up here?"

Dan rolled off some to assist swallowing and to ease the muscle control that he had brought. "Listen, Tony we need to take care of Ali. He seems on death's door. Let's take turns at being nurse and make sure he gets anything he needs." Dan felt this would also help distract McPhee from his own poor condition.

"Sure," said McPhee.

They were inside and warm. At least they had started off well. The first part of the plan had been executed, including imponderables that he had not expected, and now it was a matter of managing the rest. The aluminum camp bed frames Dan had brought up in anticipation of being here with his family in the summer were comfortable, and the foam mattresses and down duvets kept them warm.

Dan's digital watch, two years old, would serve as a calendar. Dan wondered how long the battery would last.

Dan turned the radio on but struggled to get any station except a distant unmistakable static that became a few recognizable words and then faded away. He did not care. He did not need the radio, but it would have been good to know what the local radio was saying. He grabbed a beer and turned to speak to his companions. "Well, we're here. I suppose the unit is absolutely in crisis mode below," he said.

"Will they send a rescue plane?" said Ali.

"No," said Dan. "They have no clue where to look. I had my transponder turned off."

They drank beer and settled in. Dan told his joke about the Irish pastor who warned his congregation about the evils of dancing that, especially when mixed with "devil's buttermilk" (beer), could cause people to weaken and fall into sinful ways. A joker in the congregation was heard to suggest that no one should have sex standing up, "lest it be mistaken for dancing." McPhee roared, and Ali smiled at Dan's schoolboy joke, but it lightened the mood.

It was four in the morning when they settled down to sleep.

Dan awoke at eight and was surprised to see Ali with a cup of tea. He said he was parched and very weak. Dan made some porridge, but Ali could only manage a few spoonfuls. The dog lapped up the rest. "I have called her Chandra," said Ali, "which means Shining Moon. She is a very nice dog, and I expect you to look after her," he said with a grin, wagging his finger at Dan.

"Okay," said Dan. "Anything you say. Tell me about your youth, Joe," asked Dan. He wondered why Ali would choose to be here in these basic conditions rather than at the hospice.

"Well, I was twenty when I got here. In Pakistan everything was so rigid, maybe not as rigid as people in the west think, but in reality there is only a feudal system of law for the less well off. I loved my parents very much. They had only one goal: to see me a success. They knew the only way for me was abroad. I was so entranced by this country, the freedoms and the way people treated each other. There seemed little or no prejudice toward me. I soon had my first date with a wonderful woman, and many others followed."

"I bet they all loved you," said Dan jokingly.

"But drink got to me very quickly, and you cannot have two masters."

"Tell me about it!" said Dan.

Ali continued. "I tried, and many tried with me, but in the end drink won. It has beaten better men than me. At least I know my parents now have enough money to lead a comfortable life, but they will be devastated when they learn of my death."

Their wood fire was going 24 hours a day. Hot water was supplied by two kettles permanently on the hob of the iron stoves, used for hot drinks and washing. The shower worked but was somewhat inefficient. Dan had bought up jerry cans of gasoline, but that would have to be sparsely used to generate light.

Dan cooked up bacon and beans and made more tea. He walked over to the Cherokee. The plane was in bad shape, but he didn't care. He knew he would not need it again. The damage during their night landing meant one of the wheel struts was bent. He probed around and thought that there were things he could rip out and use. The fuel he could use as well. The serious bad weather could start anytime. In the case of a bear or cougar attack, he had a rifle. He felt secure.

The dog was sniffing around the kitchen, so Dan gave her the leftovers from his and McPhee's breakfasts. "Ali calls her Chandra," Dan related to McPhee. "It means Shining Moon," Dan said in an exaggerated way. Both men laughed. The dog whimpered and slunk off.

Two days later Ali called Dan over and said he had asked God for forgiveness for his sins and his wayward life. He was very weak and only taking a few sips of water. The dog was asleep against Ali. Dan perceived that was some comfort to him. Dan had given him a powerful concoction of painkillers. Ali said that he was thankful for the life he had had, and that then said, "Look around you, Dan. Look at all the wonderful things that nature gives you. God is indeed so great. He may be unhappy with me, but it's just all so wonderful. My time has come, but it is in keeping with everything around me."

"I don't think he is too unhappy with you," Dan said to Ali, unsure where the kindness he felt for this man was coming from. "You have never hurt people, Ali. At least I would be surprised if you had. What happens to us, sometimes it's just life. We lose focus and let things happen that shouldn't."

"Thank you," said Ali. "If I had my time again, I would not waste it so badly or surrender to drink. Please, if you can, give me a funeral pyre. If not, then set me out for the buzzards to eat, like the priests do in Katmandu."

McPhee was not in good shape either but could still walk. He said, "What a guy. No moaning about his plight. He has never mentioned his illness and can see the beauty around him in things we take for granted." Both men were deeply moved.

Dan was still doing reasonably well and wondered if it was the adrenalin that was keeping him going. He did not feel too bad, relatively speaking, at all.

Ali asked Dan to draft a final letter and will that would be found if ever their camp were discovered. He apologized to his parents and reiterated his intention that all he owned was to go to them in his will. Minutes later, without further ado or discomfort, with both of his friends beside him, he slipped away from this world, exhaling one long breath.

Dan and McPhee wrapped Ali in his duvet, neither knowing what to say.

The next day Dan built a funeral pyre 30 metres from the camp and laid Ali on the wood. He layered more wood over the top of Ali's body and, McPhee standing next to him, set the pyre alight. They added more wood during the day until body and bone were mostly incinerated. Both men lamented their recent friend and his contribution to their understanding of the simple and the natural. The dog looked morose and followed Dan around wherever he went.

CHAPTER 12

Diane and the two children felt under siege, not knowing what had happened. Sergeant Squires informed her that three patients were missing but no wreckage was found. Quite frankly he told her that they had no clue where to look. A taxi driver had volunteered that he dropped off three people at a small shopping center near the airport. Those descriptions matched the three people missing from the hospice.

Squires asked Diane about Dan and what had happened in the past. He asked about Running Bear's death.

People looked at her strangely. Some had questions, and others felt grief for them but were too polite to express it. People did offer support, as did her parents. Father Smyth called from Vancouver, devastated by Diane and Emma's loss so soon after Natalie's passing, to offer condolences. Diane soon found that her grief had to be contained and only let it out quietly and when alone.

Cub spoke to her after she dropped the kids off at school and asked if she needed anything. "No," she said.

He said, "Look, I know you had lot to put up with with Dan, and I think leaving you alone with the kids while he was getting pissed all the time was wrong. From what I hear, he was pissed up in the air too!" She looked at him, open-mouthed, but he continued. "I am always here for you if you need to get away for three or four days … if you need to get away from here."

She rounded on him. "How dare you pretend to know anything about Dan? Now you listen, mister. Mind your own business!" She swung around and marched off, seething.

She got home and cried, deep sobs of grief, anger, frustration and loneliness. She wanted a proper life, and that had not been happening with Dan's drink dependency or his disappearances into the mountain wilds for days at a time. And now he had disappeared for good, as far as she could tell. But there were no textbooks for how she was to carry on with her life. She bit her lip and decided to immerse herself in her family and take things one day at a time.

Her good friend Marlene hugged her. There was nothing to say, just to be there for her friend. Marlene thought Peterson an arrogant bully. Diane made coffee and began to share her feelings with Marlene. "It's been difficult for a few years now, with Dan's depression and drinking. When we first met, he was different and seemed to have got over John's death. I think John's father absolving him of blame helped, but as time went on, he seemed to take it to heart again. He became more moody and quiet. I thought the change of job and his new occupation would mean an improvement in his temperament, a lifting of the veil of depression that seemed to befall him. We had no reason to be sorry for ourselves. We have two wonderful children, and we have more than most. No reason not to be happy. It was just so difficult to bring the subject up and get through to him. And then the ALS and his disappearance."

Marlene listened intently. She felt sad for her friend, whom she had known since they were children. "So you think this is mostly because he could not get over the death of his friend?"

"Certainly," said Diane. "I think there were people at the Manitoba Mill who blamed Dan. They were just a bunch of kids with motorbikes. John ended up hitting a grader that was driving without lights. He died on the spot. It was deemed an accident, but Dan has never been able to talk about it, certainly not to me."

A bang on the door interrupted their conversation. It was Sergeant Squires, coming to give Diane an update report.

There was no new news.

CHAPTER 13

There were wolves, bears, cougars, goats, lynx, caribou, deer and many other animals in the heights that surrounded the encampment. They all worked hard for their living during the winter and summer. Great grey owls made short work of the smaller animals like hares, rabbits, bats, chipmunks, marmots—any moving animal they could cope with. Other than animals that hibernated or couldn't survive the extra demands of grazing in the cold and snow, the others were, relatively speaking, abundant. The long winter meant a life cycle in equilibrium with nature and also meant little or nothing was wasted. Animals never disturbed the camp, but many approached, especially at night, curiosity getting the better of them. It was almost a daily saga for the duo to point out the different animals and discuss how the whole ecostructure worked. Dan presumed he would make a meal for one of the carnivorous members of the mountain club when his time came. He wondered how the poor dog would cope when he was gone.

Dan saw McPhee begin to falter; Dan's decline had plateaued. He had not felt a decline in the two months since he had been on the mountain. He wondered if he could make it till spring.

Maybe the lack of the proper drugs was accelerating McPhee's demise. He could still drink beer but suffered terribly from coughing fits. The liquid would often go down the wrong way, leaving him sputtering. Dan slapped McPhee's back and generally helped him however he could. He himself felt okay.

While was glad he had come up to his camp, he continued to feel guilty about Diane and the kids and the way he'd left, never giving them a final goodbye that they could remember him by. It gnawed on him that he had done that, and he was, not for the first time, overcome with shame and impotence. Dan felt a deep gnawing in his soul for his family. He could still justify his actions as saving them pain, but the thought of never holding his two small children or Diane was very painful. It was leaving a black void in his soul.

McPhee ribbed Dan when he was chopping wood and had Dan practice boxing moves and exercises. McPhee pretended that he would get Dan in shape so that when the two of them were okay McPhee would promote Dan and they would both become rich. It gave them both a good laugh. McPhee seemed to enjoy passing on his knowledge, even if he knew it was going nowhere.

Dan was conscious of battery life but played a Rolling Stones cassette for McPhee. The music reminded Dan of Diane. The mountain air was invigorating, and he was very glad to be in this wonderful place. He had considered moving into upper part of the control tower, but the cold soon proved too much for them. They needed to be at ground level, near the wood burners, especially the overnight stove that could last all night. He preferred to have it burn quicker and hotter, so it needed replenishing after three or four hours.

Early the next morning Dan heard the engine of a light aircraft, but he did not even check it out. There would be no rescue. He felt secure that the camp was camouflaged well enough. He was intrigued that a plane would be anywhere near here, unaware that in fact it was Bev Miller looking around for wreckage or a crash site.

Later Dan decided to leave a sleeping McPhee to check out the lake and see if there were some good ice-fishing spots. He had a small auger in the plane and congratulated himself in bringing one up. Rather than drag it and other equipment to the lake he thought he would first do a reconnaissance of the area. He took his rifle and trekked his way down to it. Dan stopped and just listened.….there was absolute silence, it was so quiet! A red tailed hawk flew by and all Dan could hear was the swish of his wings passing. Such a wonderful place with its pristine snow covered ice and contrasting rocks and firs. For some reason which he could not put his finger on Dan felt uneasy. He felt that there was someone there and quickly turned around almost expecting to see someone or some thing creeping up behind him. He felt a sort of current running through his veins. Then it was gone! Wow! Keep a grip on yourself! Everything was peaceful again.

His thoughts floated to Ali, Aunt Natalie, and Running Bear. He supposed he would be meeting them soon enough. But something did not fit in here. Something was missing as if an important component was missing. Here with his situation with the lost ones he loved with the beauty of nature and seeing it as few others had seen it and with the cycle of life and death all around him, something was missing. But what?

CHAPTER 14

t was now early December, and snow was lightly falling. Dan woke at two in the morning, the dog barking as McPhee coughed violently and struggled for air. He rushed to him and sat him up. He slapped his back to help him expel the fluids. "Don't let me drown, Buddy. Please use the gun. I don't want to spend two weeks drowning!" McPhee's cough subsided, and he fell back into a troubled sleep.

In the morning Tony "TNT" McPhee thought back to the night when he first knew something was wrong. He had gone across the pond to fight at the Albert Hall in London, England. The Albert, was named after Prince Albert, Queen Victoria's husband, was an old Victorian hall, a favorite for boxing fans, who could hire a box to watch the fight and have a waiter knock on the box door to keep them supplied with drinks during the fight.

The scheduled challenger had had to withdraw due to a training accident that left him with a torn muscle, so McPhee's management team had flown over on short notice. The super middleweight title was on the line. While it was an excellent opportunity for McPhee, he realized that he had been chosen for his current shaky form instead of more dangerous opponents. McPhee's overall win/loss ratio had been very good until recently.

The worst possible place to discover you had all but lost your ability to defend yourself was in a boxing ring when a very able boxer was coming at you. After four rounds McPhee was down four rounds. "Come on, man, that's another round you lost!" barked the irritated and annoyed Jonesy, his longtime trainer, a frown wrinkling his forehead. "That's four on the trot. You got to move forward and catch him as he counters. He's wide open for that. What's the problem?"

McPhee was bewildered about what the problem was. He was always in reasonable shape, though he had struggled in training. But he should have been able to power his way in, which was his game plan. But he could not find any strength in his arms at all. This was an opportunity for him, so he kept his mysterious lethargy to himself. He knew he was not in best shape but did not want to pass up fighting at the highest level. He was always happy to take a few shots to get a few of his own in.

The bell sounded, and his opposition, sensing victory, came out and caught McPhee with a tremendous uppercut that sent him crashing to the ropes. McPhee was out of gas. Throwing his shoulders forward, he positioned himself for an attack. A left hook caught him squarely on the jaw and dropped him to the canvas. He got to his knees but at the count of six the towel flew in over his head. His opponent jumped in the air and raised his gloves.

Eight weeks later he was diagnosed with ALS. The *Globe and Mail* headline read Boxer in His Biggest Fight.

Dan wondered how this would play out. He did not have the equipment to help keep McPhee's lungs clear. He noted that this would be happening to him before long. How to end this for McPhee? He decided the small amount of morphine he had brought for himself for his final day should be used instead for McPhee. That day would not be long coming for McPhee. Dan had other painkillers, but rather than visualize the inevitable future, he decided to take things as they came. It had served them okay so far.

Next morning McPhee was breathing deeply, relaxed. "You seem to be doing good, buddy," he said to Dan. "You seem better now than you have been since I first saw you three months ago. Keep doing those exercises, and keep chopping wood. You never know—you may make it out yet!"

Dan laughed loudly. "Well I may have plateaued out for now," said Dan. "But it's all only going one way. How are you coping?"

"Not good," said McPhee. "I don't want to go through that again. Last night was frightening and agonizing, like someone choking you and then letting a little air in and then choking you again."

"Well, I have something for you that will see you off with one shot," said Dan.

McPhee grinned. "Is that a bullet, buddy?"

"No, but it is a shot!" Dan grinned. "A shot of morphine."

McPhee visibly relaxed, knowing he could choose the timing and manner of his death. "Oh boy. Thank you, thank you, thank you. You have enough for yourself?" asked McPhee.

"Plenty," lied Dan.

"Probably not long now, buddy," said McPhee. "I feel

like I need a proper rest. I do wonder sometimes what it was all about, but up here it all seems to fit. There seems a full circle to everything, but I do have regrets … I wish I had stayed with Erica and that I could tell her things now."

"Do you want to write a few things down?" asked Dan.

"I would not know what to say," replied McPhee.

"Well, Tony, just imagine you are on the phone and she is at the other end. What would you say?"

"I would say I was an idiot and that she was everything to me and that I wish things had been different," said McPhee.

"Then write that down. It may make a tremendous difference to her in the future." Dan could see that McPhee was struggling. Dan now faced the same decision as his aunt's doctor. It was all about when.

McPhee wrote a brief note, the address in Winnipeg, to the love of his life. He told Dan he could not spell very well. Dan helped him to form this thoughts into sentences. Dan promised that whatever happened, he would leave all three final messages in the aircraft. Maybe some time in the future they would be found.

McPhee said, "I was always the hard man, the enforcer. As I grew up a bit, I took good advice to box full time, which pulled me away from the biker gang I was in and gave me some structure that was not there before. Erica's family were totally dysfunctional, as were mine. We used to argue lots but managed to settle down for a while, especially after the baby was born. But when I was at training camp her family would get at her, and eventually it fell apart. I should have tried harder and pulled my family away, but I just got fed up with it all and hit the bars. We needed to get away from our respective families or be torn apart, which is what happened."

The next attack came two days later. McPhee gasped for air and coughed violently to expel phlegm and blood from his lungs. There was little respite. He fixed his eyes on Dan's. "Now, man," he said. Dan filled the syringe with morphine, squirted a little out and gripped McPhee's arm, injecting the morphine into his vein.

McPhee smiled and quickly lost consciousness. He slipped away from this world. Dan cried a little as he said a prayer, a eulogy over his warrior friend. He had not asked McPhee about his choice of bodily departure but decided on the same as Ali's. He said a few prayers as McPhee's body burned next to Ali's pyre. He siphoned a little fuel out of the plane to increase the heat and made a wooden grave marker for his two friends.

He needed wood and knew he should add more to his considerable pile, but how long would he need it for? He rigidly kept his mind on this new high, hoping that if he could keep going he would not relapse to his previous condition. So he chopped up a load from the pile he had accumulated. Then he slept.

He was now truly alone. Dan reconfigured his camp; he and the dog were now the only occupants. He was able to make better use of the wood stove and slept close to it. The cold was now intense, winter's full force upon him. The dog slept next to Dan.

He surveyed a gully close to the camp that led to a ravine. He descended to look around. It was two in the afternoon, and he headed back to camp not wanting to get lost in the twilight or dark. As he came out of the valley, he observed a few sheep, with their scraggy coats and coiled horns just on the cusp. He would return tomorrow. The ram with the coiled horns would make good eating.

Dan left with the dog at first light and headed over the top of the hill. The mountain dipped and plateaued above a frozen lake neatly nestled in the center. Dan had a line in his pack and used his ice pick to fashion a hole in the ice. He dropped a hook, a colourful fly-style bait attached. Twenty minutes the movement of the line surprised him, and ten minutes later he pulled out a two-pound lake trout, a small one but good enough for Dan. Dan quickly replaced the bait and put the hook back in the hole. He had found another source of food that would vary his diet. After another twenty uneventful minutes, Dan pulled the line and made his way back to the gulley to hunt the ram.

He reluctantly shot an elderly ram, taking utmost care to kill the animal with a single shot. It hit the ground immediately and died instantly, as all but the very lowest of Canadian hunters insisted prey should. If the animal was giving its life so you could eat, then it should be shown every respect and accommodation. Dan thought the ram had lived well. Like Dan taking off from the hospice, the ram would not have to experience the horror of an abattoir like his contemporaries in the "civilized" world. Dan now had plenty of meat for a prolonged stay, should he need it.

Dan struggled to get the sheep back to the camp. He had considered butchering it where it lay, but he decided instead to do a proper job at camp. Dan butchered and hung the meat.

For the next six weeks, Dan and the dog lived day-to-day

lives. He made sure to keep his source of water open by hacking a new hole through the ice daily. He busied himself with surviving, rationing his food to last as long as possible. He had not thought that he would be around this long. They had left Memphis late October; next week was the first week of March. Spring in the mountains was still two months away.

Christmas had been a particularly bad time, and Dan had drunk himself into a deep depression. Dan howled and roared into the night with such horror, such pain—the deep, resounding roar of the animal he was—that many of the mountain inhabitants wondered about the unknown sound. His long shaggy hair and thick beard meant he would have blended in perfectly with the other occupants of the mountain.

He roared, his face screwed up, tears running down his cheeks, one fist clenched and the other gripping a bottle of rum. It was a defiant cry full of the injustice, pain and horror of being unable to comprehend his circumstances. Dan cried and drank himself into an oblivion that chased away the demons that visited him. He wanted desperately to be with his family but knew he had made his choice; there was no going back. If he had stayed at the hospital, then at least he could have seen them.

The severe cold settled on the unconscious man. Two small but deadly black wolves, seeing no movement in the camp, came in and moved toward Dan. Chandra barked and growled as loudly as she could, stirring and nudging Dan to consciousness before scaring off the wolves. Dan saw them scarpering off and realized he had had a lucky escape. The barking dog that had then nudged him awake had saved the day. Frozen, Dan staggered to where his fire had gone out, poured gas on the firewood and set it alight. Chandra nuzzled up against him. He was glad he had the dog there and wondered about the dog's fate. It would be difficult for a "town" dog to survive up here. He fell asleep.

The poor old Schnauzer had had no life constantly being chased off by bigger dogs and always hungry. Scraps from dumpsters and bins around the back of food establishments were her biggest provider and the cold was always there in winter. Sleeping under people's porches was as warm as it got. Many dogs froze when weakened by illness or injury and there were many ways that could happen in Memphis. Left in the woods in summer after a previous owner passed on, she was deemed superfluous by other family members and dumped. In the stray dog pecking order Chandra was indeed very, very low on the totem pole. Even some cats were prepared to chase her off! Humiliation! Her best tactic was to run beside people (particularly families) as they walked away from takeaways and give a low whimper and giving her best 'hungry dog' look. She did remember being chased off by Dan ages ago as any dog that survives in that climate needs to remember both the friendly clients and the not so friendly also. The town dog catcher had caught her once and she had been vaccinated, sterilised, fed and caged with other dogs. She managed to escape whilst being exercised off the leash by a volunteer dog walker. Many dogs ran in packs which got them into trouble and many seemed to go just mad as the bitter cold arrived continued (there was no chinooks at Memphis) and chased and barked at cars till they were eventually hit. Another version of barking at the moon. Jumping into the aircraft that night was desperation tactics but it seemed to have paid off. Regular food, warmth, and an interesting situation even if the people kept disappearing. She told herself it was an exceptional piece of good fortune.

In Memphis, Diane thought about Dan as her family celebrated Christmas. She wondered where he was and if he was alive. She wished he were there beside her.

CHAPTER 15

He had a terrible dream that he had weakened and the ALS had come on full bore. All the forest animals—bears, wolves, wolverines—came to the camp and started to devour him. He could not keep them off, and he woke screaming, covered in sweat. He fell back into an uneasy sleep, where all his past transgressions hammered away at him. He felt like he was on fire, frustrations and electricity coursing through his veins. Then he was surrounded again by the forest animals that snarled and hissed at him. He sensed Diane was there, and he sensed she was looking for him, looking to find *him*. The hairs on the back of his head began to rise. He felt something behind him, and a massive shiver went down his spine. He turned in slow motion to face Running Bear. He was paralysed. Aunt Natalie watched him, as did Ali and McPhee. A fever raced through Dan's veins. He desperately wished his friend was alive. He thought of the chasm of unendurable sorrow at his funeral, Saffron having to be physically supported by two friends, and John's parents with devastated looks on their faces. It was pure horror, minus the acceptance when people have lived long lives and their time has naturally come. John

"Running Bear" Cardinal was only nineteen when he died. Dan looked deeply into the face of his departed friend, into his smiling brown eyes, and collapsed.

"What's the matter with you, man?" said John. "My time came, as yours will. Live your life. Live your life. You got things to do, people to love." A mist shrouded them as the apparitions faded away.

He woke shouting and awash in sweat, but he felt strangely different. He was very calm. It was as if his terrible but beautiful dream had cleansed him. The fire in his veins had gone. He felt that John's death seemed to be in harmony within the backdrop of nature and the cycle of life up here. He would die when it was time for him to do so, as John had, not before. Dan saw everything from a different perspective. Being up here and believing he had only a little time left helped him gain this perspective. A strange feeling of satisfaction from being able to help both Ali and McPhee when they needed it swept over him. This time he was able to do something.

His muscle atrophy seemed to be gone, and he was ravenously hungry. He felt like he had not felt in a long, long time, like before he had come down with ALS. He washed in a bucket because his shower was kaput. He made a big breakfast and chopped more wood, lots of wood. All his power seemed to have returned. He could completely breathe in lungs full of fresh mountain air and began stretching and lightly exercising his body.

The dog, sensing change, barked and jumped up at him.

What had happened overnight? It was as if his inner being had been renewed. He felt a wonderful optimism and fortitude. Dan whooped and yelled for 20 minutes while the dog barked at him, before a voice in his head reminded him that he could soon begin a downward spiral. He sat down with his tea and digested this new dimension to the situation. He chewed his food and told himself not to get his hopes up too much. Dan felt that whatever happened from here, he had drawn a line under the past. It was as if seeing his friends die up here against the background of the natural cycle of life and having watched Running Bear die years earlier had put everything into context for him. It was not for Dan to judge or feel responsible; it was for him to get on with life.

But he had to consider the new dimension to the situation. His new objective, unless thrown back into ALS, was how to get the hell out of here. He began to work out how long it would take to hike down, but it would be dangerous, surely suicidal, to try in winter. He went to sleep quickly and had a terrible dream that he woke up back in the clutches of ALS. But when he woke his condition was still good.

CHAPTER 16

Cub Peterson was annoyed. He was having a bad day. He had gone into a rage when a new clerk became confused over some contracts and included the wrong information. He ignored the fact that she had had little training and fired her in front of the three girls in the accounts office and the accounts manager. His temper was not soothed when the fired employee told him in a few short sentences what he could do with his job and blew a raspberry at him. His underlying annoyance was that he had planned to be seriously dating Diane Owen by now, but the high and mighty Diane had snapped at him for his realistic views (in his mind) about her (he supposed) now-passed husband. Cub was sure he was the best catch in Memphis, with his dealerships, tough-guy image and good looks. Cub could not believe that anybody could resist. So he tried again to intercept Diane on the school run and took two employees with him to magnify how powerful and what a great leader he was.

He approached her as she was dropping her two children off at school. "Hi, Diane," Cub greeted as she returned to her car. Diane turned her attention to him, saying nothing.

"Diane, we are having a champagne toast to the launch of the new F-150 at midnight. I am inviting special customers and potential customers to come over. What time do you want one of the guys," he gestured to his employees, "to pick you up? Eleven okay? I will have a glass of champers waiting for you." Cub grinned his widest pearly white smile.

Diane simply replied, "No thank you," and opened the door to her car.

Cub, enraged again, said, "Too bad for you. It's not my fault that your ex flew off drunk and slammed into the side of a mountain. Maybe he had cause! Not my fault, is it? All I want to do is help. I can get any number of people I want to come to my events. Lots of girls would feel privileged to come."

Diane said nothing. She just started the engine and drove off. Cub's attack cut deep to the bone, not because of his cheap words, but because it made her feel further isolated and depressed. She knew Cub was a jerk, but the manner in which he could just send his rage at her was humiliating. She could have just screamed an obscenity at him, but it was not her style, and she would feel no satisfaction from dropping to his level.

She decided if there were one more approach from him she'd call Squires in to warn Cub about harassment.

Cub regained his cool, smiled at his two employees and said, "Let's go. We don't fucking need her."

Diane had started a part time job with the largest law firm in Memphis and quickly found that she had a talent for understanding complex cases and at what stage they were at.

Shuster Bros. consisted of Darren and Peter and neither were known for their administrative efficiencies or their ability to remember any instructions or facts if it numbered more than two. Add a third then the first would be forgotten. Both we very 'old school' and Diane's first suggestion was that they change their timing for the weekly workload in 'The Pit' (where they and Dianne would meet to ensure the cases scheduled for that week had all the documentation current and all evidence available) from Friday to Monday morning helped some of the facts to stay with them further into the week. Neither could use a computer other than in a very rudimentary way. Immediately, she began to take some online courses that could eventually lead her to become an Articled Legal Clerk. This important position needed people who were able to introduce witnesses and clients into the court system at the right time and with any documentary paperwork/evidence also. Diane enjoyed this work, and it gave her a sense of purpose and accomplishment. The two lawyers running the firm thought her a godsend and were happy to pay for any course she wished to go on and helped her formulate a career path. Their were also two legal secretaries working for the firm and both were so happy that there was someone to take the load off them, where the work had fallen after the last artcled clerk had given up on the two brothers and found employment elsewhere. One of them mentioned to Darren that this was Friday and that Diane had only a months contract which would be up by the end of the day. Panicking the two brothes quickly asked for a meeting with Diane to offer her a permanent role. She was being paid $23 per hour and whilst the two were the most frugal of frugal Peter said "Somethimes we must pay above the odds to get who will be of such benefit to us." Darren agreed so they invited Diane in and proposed an offer of a permanent position with a title of Articled Clerk Designate an a new rate of $30 per hour with a review after 3 months with a salaired position offer. Diane smiled as Peter holding his two hands out with fingers spread forward said 'Well Diane what do you think?" Darren was looking at her with his mouth wide open and saying whilst breaking into a smile " "We will of course take care of any educational cost's you have like books and courses and of course child minding avitivities". Dianne smiled and gratfully and gracefully accepted their offer, realising the main thrust of Schuster Bros would be on her desk. She was now the engine of the company. The offer was a great relief to her. She had all the traits of people living in the North that were needed to survive including grittiness, fortitude and a sense of humour but, Lord knows there was little to laugh about lately. Another thing you needed was a strong charaghter to be able to see you through the bad times, the troubled times when things looked hopeless. She had her two chrildren and now a career to keep her focused and keep the anxiety at bay. Both Darren and Peter smiled broadly and Darren said "I believe we should go out and celebrate with a luncheon at Boston Pizza"! which all five of them headed straight out to.

A month later Diane was leading the the two barristers in the court gratly increasing their abilities to just concentrate on case in hand. Her sense of self and awareness of here situation and ability to handle it grew her confidence.

Father Smyth from Vancouver had heard about Dan's disappearance from Emma and called Diane to offer condolences but also to offer any spiritual support he could.

He asked Diane's permission to get the local church to call her. Diane was aware that she was now it a different role as heading up the family and wondered what might have been if she had faced up to or rather made Dan face up to himself all those months/years ago.

*

CHAPTER 17

Dan could not remember what it was that had sent him into the depression that had caused the void between him and Diane, only that it had happened. The Stones were playing "Brown Sugar," and it took him back to the time when they had both danced to it, laughing and enjoying the closeness to one other and the fun. He remembered what he had said about what McPhee would say to Erica if she were on the phone. He asked himself what he would say to Diane.

He thought about her again and, as alcoholics did, had a moment of total clarity about where he was, who he was and what he would do if she were here now. If he had another chance at life with her. He knew that she would never pass a day again without him letting her know how much he loved her. Life without her and his family seemed desolate, even with his restored health. In fact, it made him anxious to make a plan to leave. The weather was impossible for a ground attempt, so his option was to wait out the winter, which meant two months. That was possible given the surrounding game but very, very tough. Or somehow he could fly out or get a message out, but he could think of no way to accomplish that. The plane's bent strut meant that it was lopsided. Plus he did not have enough fuel to make it back to the airfield at Memphis. He thought it through. What would Bev say? "Once you know what you cannot do, you are left with what you *can* do!"

The plane carried a parachute. He had come up here and landed in the dark; if he could take off now and get three quarters of the way back on the fuel he had, then he could bail out and take it from there. As with many things, the hardest part became easy. He inspected the bent strut. He could hammer it back reasonably easily. That meant that although the aircraft would be somewhat level, the strut could bear little strain before bending again or, worse, snapping. A welded fillet would fix it in no time, but, of course, he had no welding facilities. The battery was dead, but that also should pose little problem. His Honda generator could recharge it. If it was totally dead, the generator could start the engine directly.

So Dan's plan became to add all his remaining fuel to the Cherokee and fly as far and as high as he could and then glide as far as possible. The radio had not been operational for some time. Trying to jump from a light aircraft that was destabilized and without power while carrying a dog was crazy dangerous. He would have to make a decision whether to jump or not by assessing the terrain at the time. Gnawing at the back of his mind was what could happen if he landed in a remote, inaccessible area, where he could not walk back to town and would perish from cold and hunger.

He was anxious to leave.

Dan restored the Cherokee to the best condition he could. He cleared the runway, such as it was, of snow. He planned to take off almost over the edge of a cliff, so taking off should not pose too many problems. He pushed the thoughts of bailing out from his mind. He had so much to lose that his anxiety and nervousness were palpable. Would the strut hold up for taking off.? He had reinforced it with a piece of flat bar with a nut and bolt at either end, but it was a rough job. He didn't have enough tools, and in reality this needed to be a welding job.

Where and how would he bail out? What if the weather forced him off course?

What if, what if, what if …?

He had obviously not made provisions for a return journey. He had a map in the Cherokee for eventualities but knew exactly where he was and where he was going. He would use dead reckoning to get back to Memphis. He would have to gradually take the Cherokee to the highest efficient altitude and set it at its most efficient flight and fuel mode so to the plane would be high as possible when he ran out of fuel. He would set the flaps with as little drag as possible. He stripped out everything from inside the Cherokee he would not need, travelling only with the survival pack he would need when he bailed out. He had two thermoses of Sencha tea. Dan grinned, remembering he had needed beer and rum to get there. He was fine with tea for the return journey. He had not thought about alcohol for weeks.

He grinned again at the incredible change in circumstances he found himself in. He was full of fear and hope and a rapturous enthusiasm for life that had never, ever existed before. He was very, very excited for the future. He thought about Diane and his family but decided to get a firm grip on his emotions. Now was the time for a cool and calculating mind to evaluate the circumstances he would face. He needed a professional and analytical attitude to get home safely.

"You know what you *can't* do," he told himself, "but what *can* you do? Focus on that. You *can* fly this fucking plane out of here!"

He relaxed as he thought of his two late friends and took strength from what he thought they would say to him right now. He felt them urging him on.

Dan tucked blankets around the engine and used a small electric heater to warm it for 24 hours before he tried to start it. It was -43 degrees. Such cold ate its way into anything mechanical, electrical or organic. -43 degrees would also badly wax up the fuel. He did not want the aircraft fuel lines becoming blocked with waxed up fuel so he fitted a heater jacket as best he could around the tanks and lines. The blow heater should keep fuel and engine from getting too cold. Dan had seen people light wood fires under fuel tanks to warm fuel but he was not going to try that today! The heater in the plane was working when it last flew and Dan was not expecting it to be broken and if it was then it was. It would just have to be a cold flight.

The town of Memphis was a few hundred feet above sea level; he could better assess how far he might get when he knew how much fuel he would be flying out with. The plane had been sitting for five months, and ice was a major worry. He knew that fuel was delivered to the engine at twice the pressure needed to ensure the reservoir was always full; a bypass returned unused fuel to the tank. This eliminated ice from building up in the reservoir and ensured ice did not build up in the fuel delivery system to the engine.

He dragged the Honda over to the Cessna and attached battery cables to the battery. He left it running for half an hour. Then Dan held his breath and put the key into the ignition. He turned it, and the console lit. His heart beat faster as he looked the fuel gauge: between a third and a half. Not bad, but not enough. He took the key out. He wanted everything to be perfect before starting the engine again, if, indeed, it would start. The Cherokee was fitted with a variable pitch propeller. Depending on his requirements, he could set it to a fine pitch that was good for taking off and climbing or a course pitch that gave better value for distance. It was like the gears in a car. Fine pitch was okay for lower gears, but course pitch was the overdrive, consuming more air and thus giving more distance per engine revolution. He could not adjust it in flight, so he would have to take off in course-pitch mode.

He completed all the service requirements that could be made to the engine. He checked, oiled and adjusted all flaps, rudder and electrical systems still operating. He would be flying an aircraft in the same way as would have been done in the First World War: no direction finder, compass, radio, or weather checks. But he knew where he was and knew how to get home.

He replaced the pilot's seat he'd previously removed for his comfort and that of his recently deceased companions. He slid the key into the ignition and hit the start button. The prop turned twice, and he switched off. He tried a second time, his heart racing, and the engine fired into life on the second turn. Dan let out a roar and punched the air.

The engine ran sweetly enough. Otherwise there were only minor adjustments he could make. He allowed it to run for a minute and switched it off. He would need every cupful of fuel.

The night sky was dazzling. But his demons were alive. Seeing such beauty, he was ashamed that although Diane had given him love and such beauty, he was too tough to properly return it. Maybe he lacked the communication skills, he thought. But he did not know how to return it. She had given him two wonderful children he had not properly appreciated. If he had another chance, he would fix all that for sure, but there were rarely second chances in love. He wondered what he would say if he ever saw Diane again, or if she were here right now. She had been wonderful to him. Why had he gone down the road he'd taken?

It occurred to him that if it were not for ALS, he would not be having these clear thoughts. He was not an alcoholic, just someone who … what? Had not grown up? More likely, he had not taken the time to see the real value in life and people. A wave of deep shame overcame him. He had never taken much notice of the setting sun or the shadows against the mountains as the sun went down or the wonderful picture nature painted as the stars began to shine against the backdrop of a full moon, all encapsulated by the blue-black sky. Both of his comrades' deaths had seemed to make some kind of sense within this framework, but he could not hold on to the thought to analyze it. He thought of where he was with life and of how the future might develop.

While not consciously debating the issues and possibilities, he, in a relaxed way, allowed the thoughts to softly tease his mind. He was in love with the world and especially with all the wonderful people he had not appreciated or let down or somewhat abused, people who had tried to help him, had given him things, guided him, but he had not appreciated any of it. Diane had given him love, and he had abused it. She gave him two wonderful children, and he had not appreciated the gift.

Thoughts flowed through Dan's mind. He knew that since Aunt Natalie had begged to be allowed to die, it just did not seem right to let that happen to people. Most people would be happily unaware that a situation like that existed until it confronted them, as it had confronted Dan. Being struck down with a major disease had changed his life. His aunt's doctor had been kind and had released her as soon as he felt morally and legally able to do so. All pharmaceutical companies were maximizing their profits by charging the most they could get for their products. The licensing period varied before cheaper or generic versions arrived on the scene. He thought, *The pharmaceutical companies say they need that profit to continue to invest in research, but the oil and gas people say the same, as do all the energy companies.* Before many African countries or charitable organizations could afford the cheaper HIV drugs, an incalculable number of people had passed on. He thought of the schizophrenic patients destined to life on the streets as they spiralled into a lifestyle that would inevitably lead them to prison, where there was no treatment or trained personnel to treat them. They called it "care in the community." But it was all about money. Dan decided that if he made it back and got his life back on track, he would at least try to campaign for these people.

Right now he had other things on his mind

CHAPTER 18

Dan decided to take off next morning at first light, knowing the propeller would more efficiently grasp the moist air, allowing the course pitch greater traction. He slept deeply without dreams and breakfasted well, as did the dog. There was much to do before he ate again, if indeed he did eat again. He secured the airport as best he could, locking the kitchen and sleeping quarters. He desperately wanted to come back in the summer, if he survived, and hoped not to be alone. He looked at the graves of his two friends, where he had buried their ashes and beauty of where they lay. They were in a different place now. Dan grinned as he looked skywards and promised himself that if he survived he would write a eulogy for them and tell their relatives of their last weeks and their bravery. He would also seek out Saffron at The Pas and talk to her about his spiritual dream about Running Bear.

The rest of the maintenance issues and take-off details could wait till he was ready to go. Dan was nervous, very nervous. He had so much to lose. When he'd arrived he was in the depths of despair, very much in the face of death. He was still convinced that it was the right thing to have done, but he could not reconcile his present feelings with his past and how he had treated Diane and his family.

It was time to go.

At 7:00 a.m. he placed his survival pack and the dog into the Cherokee and hit the starter button. The engine roared to life. Dan set the throttle at a quarter open, a full, rich mixture, and adjusted the throttle to 1,000 rpm. As the engine warmed up, Dan completed a preflight check, removed the wooden blocks that acted as chocks and jumped quickly into the plane. He took a last look around. Instead of reminiscing, Dan focused his thoughts on the job at hand as he strapped himself in. He laughed and stroked the dog's head. The bent strut meant that the plane was anything but level, but Dan would take the aircraft up in any way possible, as long as it would fly. As the Cherokee thundered down the runway, Dan check the brakes and steering. He increased the engine speed to 50 KIAS and slowly, too slowly, speed increased. A voice in his head said, "We are running out of runway, we are running out of runway." Dan maximized engine speed and pulled the control column back as the plane went over the edge of the cliff. It lifted almost sideways, but he was airborne. *Wow, that was different.* He sighed with relief.

The Cherokee seemed to be in reasonable condition and chugged along wonderfully. Dan flew at 6,000 feet, setting the aircraft at cruise altitude and 75 percent power. Dan filled a cup full of green tea from his thermos. The dog looked at him and gave a bark. Despite losing his friends, he felt deliriously happy. He had never felt so optimistic.

Things were great. His fuel tank, now that the Cherokee was level, indicated it was just below half. Dan adjusted his compass and enjoyed the flight, although he was somewhat anxious, knowing he would have to bail out at some point, or crash-land. He decided he would need to make that a last-minute decision, whether forced landing or bailout.

Dan hummed along and watched the fuel gauge slowly deplete. He calculated that he had another 100 kilometres to fly and realized that he would get much closer to Memphis than he'd thought. Within half an hour, he began to make out shapes in the far distance ... a granary that had been there since the 1870s, a church spire. In thirty minutes he would be *over* Memphis! The aircraft spluttered, and Dan quickly flipped over to the reserve tank. Dan kept the revolutions at optimum. He would ensure he would not overfly any buildings or populated areas but remain above the countryside, aiming for the airport that was, conveniently for him, north of the city. A thin wisp of smoke from the engine was leaving a dark trail behind the aircraft.

CHAPTER 19

Diane was shopping with her girlfriend Marlene, checking out the offers at Hyperstore, before they sat down in the in-house coffee shop. She had lapsed into a dignified widowhood, determined to make a life with her two children and take life as it came to her. She had now settled into her new job and was coping well with her new circumstances, even if inside she was in turmoil. She supposed this was how many people who had lost loved ones faced their days.

Diane and Marlene were sipping their coffee when they saw Constable Squires drive by with what looked like vagrant sitting next to him. Both women smiled.

Dan prepared himself mentally to use the chute, but the situation had changed again. He could see the airport tower in the distance. At this height he *might* be able to take the plane in! Dan did not want to bail out with the dog tied to him; there were too many possible complications. The engine ran smoothly enough, but telltale dark smoke was beginning to pour from the exhaust. *Not a problem*, Dan told himself. If it had been present from the beginning that would have been catastrophic. The smoke thickened, and

Dan realized that he had to keep calm. He had no radio to call the control tower, no instruments to help.

In Memphis, people were beginning to notice an aircraft coming in with billowing smoke. It was a very cold morning with a wonderfully bright sun, and the contrasting silvery airplane and black smoke seemed to capture people's fascination, as if they sensed the impending danger and could only imagine the situation for those in the plane. Then a loud bang echoed as the Cherokee's engine failed.

Sergeant Squires was watching things unfold. He wondered as he jumped into his prowler and headed to the airport what had happened to his sleepy little town. It was all falling apart. Squires had always made management decisions that involved minimizing the danger in any situation and resolving a crisis with the minimum of fuss. Squires never had, in 25 years, used his gun.

Dan estimated seven kilometres remained. At three and a half kilometres, two things happened simultaneously: he ran out of fuel, and the engine blew up. A massive loud clap, like a field gun firing, erupted as it seized, followed by fire and smoke. Oil covered the windshield. Dan's heart leaped, but he quickly used the windshield washer and wiper to good effect. He could just make out the edges of the runway; he positioned the plane centrally and gritted his teeth. Smoke continued to billow from the engine, but thankfully so far with just a little flame.

Cedric was having a panic attack. He screamed down the phone to the on-duty constable, "Get up here, and bring

Goswell's fire engine *now*! Plane's coming in with no radio, and it's on fire!"

Two pilots looked on with incredulity and aborted their landing as the Cherokee with smoke billowing behind it usurped their landing slot.

The plane was now on fire. Thick black and white smoke erupted from it. Dan was counting down the height and praying he could make the runway.

As the aircraft hurtled towards the runway, Dan was on edge. He had had more than enough of everything. It all needed to happen the hard way. Nothing was easy! His decisions were matters of life or death. He yearned for simplicity and relaxation. He wanted to set his mind in float mode.

Then Dan hit the runway hard, and the bent strut immediately gave way, sending the Cherokee careering down the center of the runway, one wing sending showers of sparks in all directions. Parts flew off. As the wing collapsed, it sent the fuselage onto its side.

Inside the plane, the noise was deafening. Black smoke was everywhere, glass from the instruments splintered, perspex shattered. Bits and pieces flew everywhere before the grinding of the plane against the runway slowly came to a stop.

Squires raced the prowler along the runway behind the faltering aircraft. It came to a halt in a hissing, smoking pile. "Chandra!" screamed Dan before man and dog jumped quickly from the remaining door. Then the whole aircraft started to burn furiously. They ran straight into the jaw-dropped Squires.

Shocked, Cedric stood in awe as a longhaired, bearded

individual with a manic look on his blackened face, followed by a yapping canine, came storming towards him! The screaming fire engine arrived, and its occupants quickly went into their routine to douse the fiery wreck.

CHAPTER 20

id you hear?" asked the orderly at the hospice.

"Hear what?" said Dr. Meers.

"They say Dan Owen reappeared, looking like some mountain man—hair about two feet long and a big beard. He landed in the plane he took off in six months ago and crashed it on the runway! It blew up, but Squires got him out."

"You don't say! I cannot understand it. He has ALS," said Meers, a frown on his forehead.

"That's what I thought too!"

Marlene and Diane said goodbye as Diane lined up to buy bread rolls. "One-fifty a dozen, Diane," said Harold the baker. "And you can get some real good ground turkey over at the meat department," he continued. "Did you hear there was a plane crash at the airport?" Diane frowned as she took in the news.

As Marlene stepped outside the store she almost walked into Sergeant Squires and the vagrant. Squires knew Marlene and Diane were friends.

"Marlene," said Squires "have you seen Diane"?

"Yes she's in the store," said Marlene wondering what was going on. Dan rushed straight past Squires and Marlene into the store and bellowed........." DIANE!!"

Diane froze as heard her name being shouted with a tremendous roar and turned to see a very well built weird long haired individual shouting her name and striding towards her. Just behind him were Sergeant Squires and Marlene who looked both astonished and bemused "DIANE!" He roared again, the look in his eyes was intense to manic.....she turned around and stepped back with only astonishment keeping her from being afraid at the sight of him. The whole store came to a stop as everybody looked to see what was happening. He stepped up to her and she could smell this earthy person with the deepest blue eyes, and she put her hands up to her mouth! She knew it was him but still did not recognise him' (The muscled tone along with the weathered face and larger frame), and he said, "I have been given another chance Diane .... can you give me, us, another chance"?

The whole store, with many people who had followed Squires and Dan in also, had kept a silent, and respectful distance (but within earshot) and Squires said, "Dan calm down, calm down" and gave Diane a signal to get Dan away. "You look so wonderful," he said to her. Diane was crying and still had her hand over her mouth. Diane's first reaction was anger. For him to turn up after all this time on a Tuesday afternoon at the Hypermarket looking like vagrant and shouting defiantly made her angry.

Squires got them out of the store and into his car. He stood outside to keep inquisitive individuals away as he noted Diane's anger and wondered if she wanted Dan back at all. Diane put one hand on his shoulder and the other gripped the side of his shirt. Tears flowed down her cheeks as the emotion came out in anger and she said "Do you know what we have been through"? "We did not know what had happened" "Anything could have happened but all we had to go on was that your plane took off with you and two others, and you were dying with ALS" The pent up fear and resentment was now beginning to pour out of Diane as she spoke. Deep down Diane thought him dead. She gritted her teeth "Is that all I am worth?" "Just some footnote in your plans to be asked if you can come back on your return?" "That's all?" "That's it" Dan put his hands up in surrender fashion and just said "No" "No" "Its anything but that", "I could not figure it out before" "I know I am just stupid". He pulled her head to his chest and said "I am so sorry". He was a mess and Diane that did not want to see him in this way anymore. She knocked on the windscreen and pointed forward to Squires who got the message and jumped into the driver's seat and drove them both to Dan and Diane's house. As Sergeant Squires dropped them off he put his hand on Dan's arm and said "The other two"? Dan shook his head, and Squires nodded and went off to file his report. He made a note to post an officer at the Owen's house to discourage inquisitive locals and journalists. There would be many, many questions on this and who knows maybe even charges.

Dan followed Diane through the gate and up to the front door where Diane let him through. Chandra pushed her way in as well sensing that now was a good time to establish herself as being officially owned. 'Let me see

Danny and Emma" said Dan. "They are around Moms"."
Best got you back and cleaned up first" said Diane. She was
still angry but his condition, the mess he was in caused her
to pity him and this diffused that anger.

"Look I know just taking off like that not telling you
and the family was unforgivable but I could not put everyone
through the cycle of watching me die piece by piece or that's
what I thought would happen" "I don't know why I am not
dead, but I am just happy to be here" "Whatever happened
to me there was transformational and I just want to begin to
live a proper life with you and our two wonderful children"
"I will be honest as I don't know myself how the change has
come about other than I am, happy in my own skin now and
want to make you happy in a way I have not in the past" "
I see a wonderful future for us if you can, hour by hour day
by day rebuilt something with me'. Diane had never heard
him speak so lucidly before, but still a little confused and
not fully confident, she reached out for his hand. "Why did
you not just call me or let me know where you were" "You
know I think I am worth that and our children are worth
that" replied Diane "I had no way to contact anybody" said
Dan. "I had no way down and no thought of it as I did not
think I would survive" "You don't seem ill any more" she
said "It makes no sense Dan" Dan put his arm around her
and said "Let's take it for what it is for now, and see what
we can rebuild" "Can we do that?" She looked at him and
smiled, the sincerity of his words disarming her hurt and
anxiety. "Yes *maybe* we can do that" she said softly. "And if
I just cannot reconcile all this Dan and just cannot live with
you"? 'Well you gave me love and two wonderful children
so I would just have to say thank you and I will support the

family in any way I can" Her anger was slowly, very slowly abating as she realised he was back." "But we cannot have the same as we had in the past Dan. Things have changes, I have changed and you seem to have done so as well". "Let's get you in the shower now," she said, "you smell…. well different. You are a pretty stinky Mister" She pushed Dan in the shower peeling off his filthy clothes and pushed him under the hot water, and he stood transfixed at the luxury of it (his shower up in the mountains having become unusable months ago) She put a tablet of soap into his hand as the steam rose all around them. Dan held her hand, and began to gently pull her towards him. "Dan, "she said quietly, but she allowed him to draw her to him under the shower and they kissed. Both of them were emotionally played out. They just held each other just enjoying the moment, trying to allow the shock of what had happened to be absorbed. She had never been so intensely moved by him. She was still a little angry and a little confused and hit Dan's chest softly with her fist but he stroked her hair and continued to draw her to him. He undressed her under hot water and held her close to him, she feeling his taut, muscular body and that intimacy that she had not felt so powerfully and had missed for so long. Dan was also in heaven. Their minds met as they made love passionately and with such intensity that only emotional hurt, pain and love can bring.

An hour later. They were dried and in dressing gowns. He was starving, and Diane was feeding him simple bison burgers and beans meal whilst he was both eating and recalling where he was and the very basics of what had happened "Where did the dog come from?" she asked, Dan recited the story of Chandra stowing away and on how Ali had adopted her. Diane also fed the dog the same stew. "If I remember that's the dog you chased off last year" Diane said laughing. "She saved my life" said Dan as he ate, Diane put her arms around him and said, "You have lots to answer for Mr." "Yes," said Dan.

"You have been away for over six months and has just come back looking like a cross between a mountain man and a hippy and I am telling you that you are not going away again any time soon!" "So we are back," said Dan 'Your damn right we are," said Diane "there was only ever us, and I think you owe me" she humorously furrowed her brow and pointed at him." They hugged and kissed, and Diane said" Remember one day at a time" "We both have changed" Diane began to laugh, "Well Well" she said and hugged and kissed Dan. She had never seen him like this never felt his personality so, so, well powerfully present and passionate!

"Let's get you dressed and over to Mum and Dads to see the kids". "No time to get you to the barbers, we can do that later and besides I want to show the whole town this madman I have back". Dan smiled and remembered his promise he made to ensure she knew she was loved both emotionally, physically and spiritually. He wondered how he could ever live without her.

She was quietly aghast in a good way at the change in Dan....how lucid and intense he had become and the change in him physically. She pulled out some of the looser of his old cloths and fed him more bison stew with beans which he was ravenously chomping down. She was unconsciously thoughtfull, things could be good but she wanted no more similar experiences. The phone rang, and it was her Mom. "Diane!" "We just heard that some lunatic appeared and that you were attacked in the supermarket, what Happened" "Its OK Mom" said Diane, who thought better of taking Dan over to her parents "you better come over and bring the kids and Dad" "But what has happened" ...." You will see Mum"!

Diane led Dan down to the basement where she figured he would have some privacy with the kids, and she would explain to her parents as much as she knew. She realised this would be more than newsworthy and that they would need to go away awhile.

Emma was shy with Dan for about three minutes. The dog expected attention and was given it by the children, and a madhouse ensued. Emma loved Dan chasing her around, pretending to be a grizzly bear. Kids being kids, there was no need to explain Dan's reappearance, although Danny Junior would need time to properly reintegrate with his dad. Diane knew that reintegration here in Memphis was not going to be easy and sensed that this wonderful honeymoon would have to, well, if not end then certainly change. She and her Mom each had a different version of the future. In Diane's mind it was a matter of how the future would emerge. Her Mom had not broached it but was seeing the situation along the "if" lines. Diane realized that, as the media circus built up and Dan's story unfolded, it might be best to move and restart elsewhere, where they could be Mr. and Mrs. Normal and their young family.

The palliative unit doctors and ALS experts and police

clamoured to see Dan. The doctors wanted to conduct tests and the police to find out what had happened on the mountain and what became of Dan's associates, the "escapees". Dan gave Squires a basic account of what had happened to McPhee and Ali and assured him that both had passed on, that both had left letters for their families on the mountain. Dan had thought it best to leave them there in case he failed to return to Memphis. He explained how they had ambushed him as he left the hospital. Dan did not mention his help in ensuring neither had suffered.

"You have to understand that it's not easy to die, but it's worse for those who have to watch the process unfold and carry on right to the end. The reason I flew up there was to save them that experience," said Dan, the emphasis on *experience*.

"I understand, Dan," said Squires. "It's good to see you back."

Squires took the statement and decided not to ask Dan about his reemergence as a person. But Squires made a mental note to save that question for the future. But now was now, and both Dan and Diane needed time together with the two children to reintegrate as a family.

The idea passed through Diane's mind that they had never been integrated before, so this was new. She saw an almost feverish streak in Dan that was not there before, an intensity for enjoying every moment. There was optimism where there had been pessimism and a wonderful outpouring of passion in their relationship that was never there previously. There were plans to make; there were things to do. There was a *future*!

Diane quickly brought Mum and Dad into her vision

for how she thought their future would roll out. While this was accepted, it was accepted with the usual reservations that went along with most things that involved Dan. They would be surprised, Diane hoped.

Dan's relationship with his two children also changed fundamentally. He seemed to be unpeeling the onions of their distinct personalities: talking, asking their opinions on things, finding out what made them tick, and generally allowing them the space to communicate with him. Before he had been generally brooding, but he was now at peace with himself and needed to connect and understand other people.

They had three wonderful days at home before Dan had to remain overnight at the palliative unit for a full medical. A quick check by the on-call doctor had the doctor scratching his head.

"Can't see or feel anything at all wrong with this man," he said.

At the unit he was probed, had many samples taken, his heart monitored, underwent an MRI, but he was found to be in excellent shape, good to go 12 rounds. They could not explain what had happened to him, except that the initial diagnosis must have been incorrect. The original samples and data would need to be reevaluated. Dr. Meers was staggered by the new Dan. He thought that he might have had an as yet unknown virus with similar symptoms to ALS that had cleared up.

Diane picked up the phone, grinned and passed it to Dan. "You still running those guns to the Irish?"

"Bev, it's great to hear from you."

"Well, sounds like you have some great adventure stories to tell, according to what I read in the paper. Catch you next week when I am in Memphis."

CHAPTER 21

The next day they drove to Dawson City, two hours from Memphis, and stopped at the superstore to shop for groceries. They were spotted by Cub, who happened to be visiting his Carson showroom. He, along with two of his employees, strolled over toward them as they were loading the groceries into the vehicle.

"Well, well, lookee here," said Cub, grinning.

Dan turned and grinned at Cub, but he picked up straight away the look on Diane's face.

"What do you want, Cub?" she asked.

"Only to say hello and welcome back," said Cub.

"Thanks," said Dan, suspicious when he observed Diane's coldness to Cub.

"Must have been hell," said Cub, "stuck up on that mountain … if that's where you were all this time." He grinned at his two buddies.

"Were did you think I was, Vegas?" said Dan, noticing the sarcasm and aggression in Cub's voice.

"Don't know," said Cub, raising his eyebrows. "Maybe you just wanted to get away, or maybe you have a whiskey

109

still up there in the mountains and were just getting pissed," said Cub with a humorless laugh.

"Well maybe you should just piss off and mind your own business," said Dan, "*after* you have apologized for upsetting my wife." He returned the humorless laugh.

"Let's go, darling," Diane said to Dan, fearing he would be hurt.

"No," said Dan with a grin. "These clowns don't bother us."

"Think you're a tough guy now, eh? You gonna stay with him, Diane?" sneered Cub, the gloves now off.

Cub had not noticed Dan's chiselled body and lean frame and could not have known about his hardened muscles, honed with axe work and the hardships of running a mountain camp. Dan had also picked up much from McPhee's boxing lessons. He took one step toward Cub, at the same time unleashing a powerful right hook that connected full flush on Cub's jaw. It dropped him to the tarmac. Cub rose and walked into the same fist, dropping him again. Straight away one of Cub's buddies came at Dan, who absorbed blows left and right but managed to uppercut him. That left just one goon standing, who thought better of it and backed away, his hands raised and pointed forward.

The first goon came at Dan again. Dan was staggered by a massive punch to the jaw and another blow to the rib cage before he caught Cub's goon with a punch to the solar plexus, ending the fight. Cub rose again but ran into a powerful right cross. They all heard a snap as his nose was broken. Cub signalled. Enough.

Cub sat on the tarmac, bemused. All his life he had had someone else fight his battles for him: his well-off parents, buying his school friends, hiring tough guys at work who would always agree with him and enforce his arguments against the odd dissenter. But now he was alone and had come up short. He made a mental note to fire the individual who had elected not to fight.

"Let's go, darling," Dan said with a soft smile, opening the door for Diane and guiding her elbow as she lifted herself into the old truck.

He reversed out, missing the chastened Cub, who had risen onto his feet and was using his hat to brush off the dust. Blood dribbled down his face.

Dan touched his hat in a goodbye and good riddance to Cub.

Diane looked over tearfully, and he put his hand on hers. No explanation was necessary.

"Honey," he said, "I need to take you and our two lovely offspring on a four-week camping trip up in the mountains as soon as the snows are gone and the kids have some holidays. I think I know the exact place to go."

Printed in the United States
By Bookmasters